A Pearl Seeker

The kingdom of heaven is like a merchant seeking fine pearls, and upon finding one pearl of great value, he went and sold all that he had and bought it.

—Matthew 13:45–46

BY JENNIFER BLACKMON STEWART

LORD HELP ME

A Pearl Seeker

Becky Blackmon

Publishing Designs, Inc.
Huntsville, Alabama

Publishing Designs, Inc.
P.O. Box 3241
Huntsville, Alabama 35810

Second Printing, February 2018

Third Printing, November 2023

Designer: Crosslin Creative
Images: dollarphotoclub.com, vectorstock.com

Editor: Peggy Coulter

Printed in the United States of America

Publisher's Cataloging in Publication Data

Blackmon, Becky, 1948—

A Pearl Seeker / Becky Blackmon.

(Lord Help Me)

1. Biblical Research—Christianity. 2. Accountability—biblical teaching. 3. Christian women—spirituality.

I. Title. II. Series.

ISBN 978-0-929540-95-5

248.8

Dedication

This book is dedicated most of all to my Father in heaven who is my Helper, my Rock, my Strength, and my Refuge. What would I do without You, my Father? Thank You, O God, for loving me.

To my precious Jeff, my forever friend.

To my children: Jennifer and Tim, Jeffrey and Angela. I love you, adore you, and cherish you.

To my precious grandchildren: Will, Nora, Max, Eva, and Lex. You simply make my world go around and around. I pray that you will be Pearl Seekers and live for the Lord all the days of your lives.

And in memory of Mom, Lea Fowler. You were the one who taught me to be a Pearl Seeker.

Becky and Jeff

Acknowledgments

Special Thanks

To my "soul sisters." You know who you are.

To the prayer warriors in my life.

To Trent, my own personal computer technician. Thank you for dropping everything and rescuing this old woman.

To Michelle, the sweetest photographer I have ever known.

Endorsements

Do you struggle with spiritual direction? Do you fall more times than you remember getting up? Becky Blackmon relates and compassionately enables us to become, "a woman for all seasons," seeking and struggling daily to please and praise our Father. In *A Pearl Seeker,* Becky invites us to walk with her through life's challenges. She relates to our falling, getting up, and falling again; yet getting up stronger each time as we grasp His outstretched hand.

—***Bremda Birckholtz***, Brandon, Florida

Becky Blackmon looks at the Bible with the fresh eyes of a Pearl Seeker, one who "digs deeply into the Word." This study is full of hope and encouragement. It has touched me and enriched my life. It is a book of love.

—***Becky Bullough***, Hanford, California

After the emotional strength gained from *The Begging Place,* I wondered where Becky Blackmon would take us next. And she has done it again! *A Pearl Seeker* inspires us to dig deeper for the pearls of God's Word and gives us women the incentive to search for jewels to help us grow more useful in His kingdom.

—***Betty Bender***, Columbia, Tennessee

As a tour guide Becky is extraordinary. She knows intimately where to take us, because she's been there before. Her excitement is catching, as she urgently leads Pearl Seekers in search of God's strength, "the good part," and a spiritual mindset. *A Pearl Seeker* will enrich your heart and touch your soul.

—***Phyllis Green***, Oakhurst, California

A Pearl Seeker calls out to straying and negligent Christians, "Change your spiritual life from drab and dull to delight and devotion." It inspires the reader to stretch for deeper understanding of the Bible.

—***Larry Acuff,*** Lithia Springs, Georgia

Contents

Preface
Lord, Help Me!

I have an ongoing conversation with the Lord. I pray all the time, and I pray everywhere. Sometimes I feel like I am a living, walking, breathing scripture—1 Thessalonians 5:17—which simply says three words: "Pray without ceasing."

And that is what I do. I pray in the car; I pray as I cook; I talk to the Lord in the middle of the night; I communicate with the Lord continually; He is my constant 24/7 companion. He goes with me wherever I go and is involved in every aspect of my life. He walks with me through the good, the bad, and the ugly! He sees it all and knows it all.

There are occasions when I fling myself at His feet in moments of sheer desperation, realizing what Hebrews 4:16 truly means: "Let us therefore draw near with confidence [boldly] to the throne of grace, that we may receive mercy and may find grace to help in time of need."

My life is imperfect to the point that I feel every day is my time of need! I need grace, I need help, and I need God. Girls, I simply need God's help—all day long!

A WOMAN LIKE ME

There is a woman from the New Testament that reminds me of me. Let's look at her.

> And a Canaanite woman from that region came out and began to cry out, saying, "Have mercy on me, Lord, Son of David; my daughter is cruelly demon-possessed." But He did not answer her a word. And His disciples came and implored Him, saying, "Send her away, because she keeps shouting at us." But He answered and said, "I was sent only to the lost sheep of the house of Israel." But she came and began to bow down before Him, saying, "Lord, help me!" And He answered and said, "It is not good to take the children's bread and throw it to the dogs." But she said, "Yes, Lord; but even the dogs feed

> on the crumbs which fall from their masters' table." Then Jesus said to her, "O woman, your faith is great; it shall be done for you as you wish." And her daughter was healed at once (Matthew 15:22–28).

What an outstanding account! Can't you just see this Gentile woman following Jesus and His apostles, shouting and pleading with them for help? She is no quiet woman. (I'm not either, so I can really understand this scene!) The apostles are probably embarrassed by her and even tell Jesus to send her away. She is not their kind.

But the Master Teacher, as usual, sees the lessons that must be taught in the most obvious and obscure places with the most obvious and obscure people. He knows what His apostles are thinking, what the woman is thinking, and what He will say and do. The Master always knows the Master plan.

Most impressive is the fact that the Canaanite woman is not afraid to approach Jesus and His inner circle of men. Neither is she fearful of pleading her case in the presence of the Almighty Judge. All she knows is that her daughter is suffering from an excruciating demon possession, and Jesus is the only one who can help her. He is her only hope.

THREE LITTLE WORDS

Desperate times call for desperate measures, and she lives in desperation every second of every day! She calls out to Jesus, "Have mercy on me, Lord—Son of David!" She knows who Jesus is even if the Jews and His apostles don't. Jesus tells her that He was sent only to the lost sheep of Israel. His words don't faze her—she only presses harder. She flings herself at His feet, bows before Him, and worships Him. And then she says these three little words: "Lord, help me."

"It is not good to take the children's bread and throw it to the dogs." This is quite bold of Jesus to say. The Jews themselves called the Gentiles dogs.

Once again this doesn't stop her. She is on a life-and-death mission. Her reply shows her great persistent faith in who Jesus really is—the

Master. "Yes, Lord; but even the dogs feed on the crumbs which fall from their masters' table."

The word she uses for dogs is the same Greek word that Christ uses. The word means little dogs or puppies. Here she is, a woman of little importance but possessing a great faith. She is also very astute and quick-witted, as she refers to herself as a little dog—using His words. She may be small and just a woman—and a Gentile at that—but she is determined to get Jesus' attention and help. Why? Because Jesus is the only one who can help her. She is at the very end of her rope. She has nowhere else to turn. She is a woman and a mother—and she loves her child with every ounce of her being. There is not a mother on this planet who doesn't understand this kind of determination or this kind of love.

Jesus commends her: "O woman, your faith is great; be it done for you as you wish." The daughter was healed immediately because of her mother's tremendous faith.

ONLY GOD

Tell me, what is it like to have a child wrapped in the arms of a demon? What is it like to look into the eyes of evil every second of every day? What was this woman's life like, and more than that, what was her daughter's life like? How does one live like that? You and I don't even begin to have a clue, my sister.

How absolutely agonizing demon possession was! In Mark 9:17–27 God gives us the account of a man whose son was demon possessed. The demon often threw the boy into the fire or water to destroy him. This father was desperate, and he said to Jesus, "But if you can do anything, take pity on us and help us!" Who are the *us* the father was referring to? Surely it was the man and his family. They all must have suffered with this child. What a never-ending nightmare! We cannot even imagine their agony. It is certainly true that the events that affect us personally affect the entire family. If the Canaanite woman had a family, they certainly were experiencing a horrible existence. How could they possibly live a normal life?

What was it again that the Canaanite woman cried to the Savior? "Lord, help me!"

Why is this woman's story in the Bible? Why is such a small encounter in Jesus' life so hugely important to you and me? Because we understand her. We can totally identify with her. Sometimes I am so overwhelmed by my life and its problems that all I can do is fall on my knees like she did, worship my God like she did, and say over and over, "Lord, help me!" like she did.

There certainly have been heart-rending occasions with my own children when I needed His help! Don't you also identify with this woman? She is a woman for all seasons, all ages, all times. She loves her broken child and needs Jesus' help. She is you and she is me.

This Gentile woman of long ago realized that only God could help her. Only God could cure her daughter. Only God could change everything. Only God.

Have you ever been that desperate? You know what I am saying. Oh, girls, we seek the Lord because we need His help! We seek the face of God because He is the only one who can heal and repair our lives. He has all the answers and the right prescriptions!

We all need help. There is no perfect life, no perfect parent, no perfect child, no perfect family, and no perfect church. We all have challenges, problems, and heartaches.

I tell my sisters frequently that I don't know how God has time for them and their troubles. He has His hands full just solving all my problems and making Becky behave! But God is God, and He can do the impossible. Matthew 19:26 tells us so. Thank God for God!

Dad used to say, "With God even the impossible is possible!"

As we begin this series, may we ask for God's help for each step we take.

Write your personal goal for this study below.
Help me, Lord,

____

Pearl Drop

I Want to Be a Pearl Seeker

I have been on a quest all my life. Have you? Don't we all want to know who God is and why we are here on earth? We search to find the right answers and the true meaning of life and where we fit in the whole scheme of things.

Life is tough, and it surely is unfair. The world is unkind, unforgiving, and unloving—the very opposite of our God. That is why we need God. He is holy and righteous, the epitome of love. We need help just to live and to live rightly. Christians need the Lord all the time. He is a God for all ages and times—a God for all the storms, all the joys, all the roller coaster rides, and all the ordinary events of our lives.

And God, being God, always provides. What a mighty God He is! Let's look at two scriptures that describe our Creator. I call the first reference the Superman Scripture. The second is from the Hebrews writer:

1. Deuteronomy 33:26–27: *There is none like the God of Jeshurun, who rides the heavens to your help, and through the skies in His majesty. The eternal God is a dwelling place, and underneath are the everlasting arms.*

2. Hebrews 13:5–6: *For He Himself has said, "I will never desert you, nor will I ever forsake you," so that we confidently say, "The Lord is my helper, I will not be afraid. What will man do to me?"*

When the Gentile woman of Matthew 15 pleaded with the Lord, "Help me!" that's all she could say. And Jesus helped her. This Gentile woman right here and now, called Becky, makes that same plea, "Lord, help me," and He comes to my aid over and over and over. His promise rings true: He has never forsaken me.

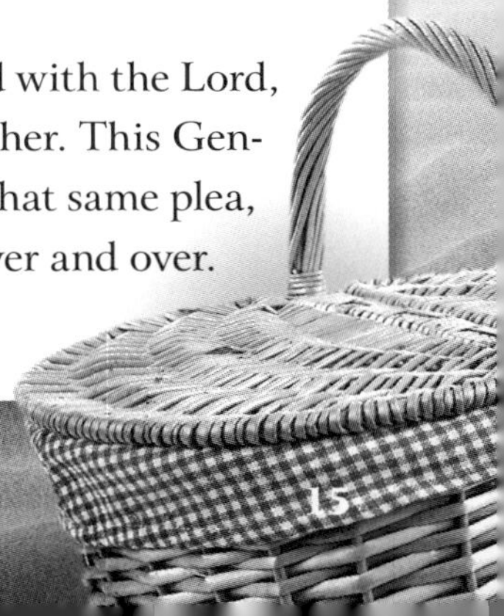

God always keeps His promises. He has never lied to you or to me. I know about the Begging Place. The Lord meets me there, helps me there, answers my prayer, comforts me, and leads the way.

This book is literally my plea: "Lord, help me!" I will always seek His help because my daily prayer is to be the daughter He wants me to be, the child He had in mind before I ever came to be. I am a Pearl Seeker.

This is a quest of a lifetime. God freely and plainly reveals all the answers to our questions in His most precious book, the Bible. Will we read it, search and study it, and delve into its deepest depths? It is up to you, and it is up to me.

Come and go with me, my sister. Let's ask, seek, and knock. Let's be Pearl Seekers.

CHAPTER 1

Seek
The Lord and His Strength

Seek the Lord and His strength; seek His face continually (Psalm 105:4).

Again, the kingdom of heaven is like a merchant seeking fine pearls, and upon finding one pearl of great value, he went and sold all that he had and bought it (Matthew 13:45–46).

Are you a Pearl Seeker? Does the thought of buried treasure intrigue you? Do you like to ask a lot of questions? If you are nodding your head, then you and I are in the same boat!

Most of us like to learn; some of us even love to learn. Those three words, *back to school,* were never my favorites; however, I do believe that attending school offers structure, higher learning, discipline, and the opportunity to sit at the feet of some unique teachers, all of which are good for children and adults alike, with few exceptions.

In every school setting, from the primary school level all the way to the college level, I remember teacher after teacher always urging us: "Never be afraid of asking questions; that is the way to learn." Learning to ask why, when, how, and where has opened so many fascinating and challenging doors of study for me. And I still ask these questions constantly.

Stimulating the brain to learn, inquire, and attain knowledge is an important task for all

Read pages 11–14, and make sure to write your personal goal for this study.

humans. It helps us live longer. We all really do like the challenges learning offers.

ANSWERS FOR INQUIRING MINDS

God, the Creator of the universe and all things, has designed the human brain to seek, to question, to inquire, and to learn how this world came into existence and how life was began. Our minds even ask, "Who is in charge?" We want to know! We observe the world, its life-forms, its ecosystems, and the universe so exquisitely set into motion. Then we ask those questions again: how, why, when, where, and who?

God answers with these simple words: "In the beginning God created the heavens and the earth" (Genesis 1:1). How simple and yet how profound. "In the beginning God . . ." Let us look at three study Bibles and hear from a few experts on Genesis 1:1.

1. *The NKJV Nelson Study Bible*: "'In the beginning' is a thesis statement which can be paraphrased: Here is the story of God's creation of the heavens and the earth."

2. *The NIV Study Bible*: "In both its Hebrew and Greek forms, the title of Genesis appropriately describes its contents, since it is primarily a book of beginnings."

3. *The Daily Bible in Chronological Order*: "Is it possible to imagine a time when no material things existed? Take away the brilliance of the sun by day, and the beauty of the moon and stars by night. What would life be like without them? Take away the clouds and sky and rivers and oceans. Imagine the earth without humans, animals, fish, birds, grass, trees, or plants. What would it be like if the earth were completely bare? Indeed, what would it be like if there were no earth, no universe—nothing? Has the universe existed forever? Surely it must have had a beginning. How did it happen? What made it happen? For what purpose did it happen? Who am I? Where did I come from? Why am I here? Since recorded history began, men

and women of every generation, culture, and place have searched for answers to those questions."

Now observe a few words about creation from the website of James Burton Coffman, a Christian commentary writer, and Frank Chesser, gospel preacher and writer:

> There is absolutely nothing either unreasonable or hard to understand about this. That there was indeed a beginning of our universe and the world we live in is absolutely certain. No matter how far back into the mists of prehistoric time men may postulate the point of origin for our universe, it is precisely there that they must confront God, the omnipotent, eternal, all-pervading, omniscient First Cause, known to Christians as the God of the Bible. This says nothing at all of when the beginning occurred, but declares emphatically that there was indeed a beginning, a fact which no reputable science on earth has ever denied. The source of that beginning was in the will and the power of the Eternal God. It was not merely a beginning of life, or of material things, but a beginning of all things (Coffman, *Genesis*).
>
> "In the beginning God . . ." (Genesis 1:1). What an affirmation! The feeble, finite mind of man reels and staggers under the load of this single thought. It is unfathomable in its content, immeasurable in its magnitude, and incomparable in its inclusion . . . "In the beginning God . . ." (Genesis 1:1). The Bible does not argue for the existence of God; it simply announces it. The first four words of divine inspiration mark the commencement of time and an introduction to the greatest Being in all that is (Chesser 9–10).

DIRECTION FOR A SEEKER

Man begins to read Genesis 1, and the journey begins. The questions begin and one's faith is born. The story of the creation of all things is the beginning of the greatest story ever told. It starts with Genesis 1:1, and it ends with Revelation 22:21.

Where do we go to seek the face of God? Where will we find answers about what He is like and how He exists? Where do we begin? Do we go to the library and see what men have written about the Creator? Do we become the woman on the street, questioning the passersby, gathering their personal opinions on religion and then deciding which faith we like best? No, there is only one place where God tells us about Himself and His plan for all mankind. The Bible! The Bible is God's book on God. A preacher once said, "The Bible is our window through which we see God."

In His marvelous Book of Books, God has issued a challenge to all mankind: "Seek the Lord and His strength; seek His face continually" (Psalm 105:4).

> Only the Bible can speak to the mind of man. The Bible is the mind of God in verbal form. It discloses the way God thinks. It addresses man's intellect, the thinking, reasoning, contemplative aspect of man's nature. God designed the mind of man (Chesser 7).

GOD IS NOT HIDING!

God reveals Himself through the written word. He makes a promise to the Pearl Seeker when He says:

> "For I know the plans that I have for you," declares the Lord, "plans for welfare and not for calamity, to give you a future and a hope. Then you will call upon Me and come and pray to Me, and I will listen to you. And you will seek me and find Me when you search for Me with all your heart. And I will be found by you," declares the Lord . . . (Jeremiah 29:11–14).

We can find God! He does not hide from us. God is completely accessible! But notice that this passage contains a condition on our part. God says that we will find Him when we search for Him with all our hearts. It is either all or nothing at all with God! Someone once said, "A half-hearted Christian cannot serve a wholehearted Savior!"

God has exquisitely arranged His brilliant Word with infinite treasures, ready to be revealed to students of all ages and types. From the genius to the simple minded, and from a senior citizen to a young child, there is something for everyone to learn from the Good Book. There is a treasure to be cherished on every page for every heart.

Augustine, a fourth-century philosopher and theologian, once described the Bible this way: "The Holy Scriptures are our letters from home." How often have we considered the Word to be a letter from our Father in heaven? A personal message from the Creator to the created? Would that view of it make us want to read it more? Wouldn't we treasure it to a greater extent? Girls, I want to seek Him. I want to find Him. I need Him more and more each day to guide my life.

A BOOK TO CHERISH

Do you cherish your Bible? Do you take care of it? I cannot tell you the number of Bibles that flew off our car's roof as we drove away from the worship service, because a certain son of ours had a habit of placing them there while he got into the car.

Have you heard the old, old story of the lady who invited the preacher for supper? To impress him, she told her little girl, "Go and get the Good Book that Mama dearly loves." The little girl returned with the Sears and Roebuck catalog!

Did you hear about the Christian painter who specialized in house interiors? He complimented the lady of the house regarding her ornate Bible, gracing her coffee table in the living room. "Ma'am, I see that you have the most important book in the world on your coffee table."

"Oh, yes, I do!" she replied. "It contains all the names, births, marriages, and deaths of my ancestors written down on its special pages. Why, what in the world would we do without that?"

Talk about clueless! That lady had no idea about God, His Word, and His message to all mankind. Her Bible was precious because of its pages with family events and dates written on them. She hadn't even read God's message on the other pages!

It remains a truism: The Lord knows how important the Bible is to each of us, whether we cherish His Word or not.

IF AND *ALL*

Whose responsibility is it to seek God? It is ours and ours alone. He certainly will not force us to find Him. A paraphrase of Proverbs 3:6 is "Seek His will in all you do, and He will show you which path to take."

What a comforting passage! Why? Because we don't even know where to walk or how to get there without guidance. But our God will demonstrate the right way *if* we seek His will in *all* things. "A man's way is not in himself, nor is it in a man who walks to direct his steps" (Jeremiah 10:23). Again, "There is a way which seems right to a man, but its end is the way of death" (Proverbs 14:12).

So what do I do? How do I find my way? How in the world am I going to know how to live right and please God? How am I going to know the truth? As Brother Marshall Keeble often said, "Get in the Book!" and "The Bible is right!"

And that is the bottom line to living here on this earth. We have to open the Bible and read what God has set before us. We must open our ears, eyes, and heart to the Lord and see what He has to say. Remember, He is our Creator with all the answers!

Underline the benefits of the attributes of the Lord from the passage below.

Make me know Your ways, O Lord; teach me Your paths. Lead me in Your truth and teach me, for You are the God of my salvation; for You I wait all the day . . . The secret of the Lord is for those who fear Him, and He will make them know His covenant. My eyes are continually toward the Lord, for He will pluck my feet out of the net.

—Psalm 25:4–5, 14–15

> I will instruct you and teach you in the way which you should go; I will counsel you with My eye upon you (Psalm 32:8).

> Your word is a lamp to my feet and a light to my path. I have sworn and I will confirm it, that I will keep Your righteous ordinances (Psalm 119:105–106).

Oh, my sisters, God's lamp still shines and guides the seekers to a magnificent life with Him, and that is just the beginning. I want to seek Him and let Him show me the way! I need Him to instruct me, teach me, and guide me all the way home because I do not always know what is best for me. I don't know where my footsteps should go, but He does. The Father always knows best. Will we confirm and vow to keep His commandments, as David did?

QUEST FOR TRUTH ALONE

Is there such a concept as truth? In his blog, Jeff Jenkins said this about the Word:

> Dr. Luke told Theophilus that he had investigated carefully everything about the life of Jesus. He further told this man whose name means "one who loves God" that he was writing it down so that he could know the exact truth about the things he had been taught. Wow! What about us? Have we carefully investigated the life and teachings of Jesus? One other thought. Regardless of what many say, it is crucial that we know the Truth. It is crucial that we be exact in our knowledge of the Truth. And it is crucial that we compare everything we are taught, everything we hear, and everything we read with the Truth found in God's Word. From Luke's opening statement about the life of our Savior, it surely appears that the Holy Spirit believes that Truth matters!

When involved in a study of the Word of God, we are on a quest for the Truth and the Truth alone. We must stop and ask the questions popping up in our heads as we read the Bible. We must look at concordances along with Hebrew and Greek dictionaries, get out maps, and follow the places God has woven into His story.

In my mind I hear Elsie Huffard's voice encouraging women repeatedly: "Make the Bible come alive!" She was a marvelous teacher and mentor to me and to so many other women who embraced Bible study. I often tell women: "We must put on our Greek glasses, Roman togas, and Jewish sandals when we study the Bible, so that we will understand what was happening when Jesus walked on this earth."

We must challenge our brains and minds to dig deeply into God's holy Word because it simply is fascinating. There is nothing like it! Well, of course there is nothing like the Bible. It is from God. No other book can make that claim. The Word of God is ground zero. This is where we begin.

> All Scripture is inspired by God and profitable for teaching, for reproof, for correction, for training in righteousness; so that the man of God may be adequate, equipped for every good work (2 Timothy 3:16–17).

The word *inspired* carries an image. It means "God breathed"—from the lips of God. The Greek word for this inspiration by God is *theopneustos*. Can't you picture God leaning down from heaven and breathing His words into the minds of men?

Furthermore, let's note another lesson from this passage in 2 Timothy. Scripture helps us teach, warn, correct, and train ourselves and others to do rightly, so that we can be equipped and ready for every good work that we are called upon to do. It sets our course.

I heard preacher Richard Harp say: "The scriptures are profitable for teaching—what is right! For reproof—what is wrong! For correction—how to get right! For training in righteousness—how to stay right!"

Does 2 Timothy 3:16–17 say that the Bible is inspired so we can be a dynamo in the business world or so we can climb the ladder of success and make lots of money? Is the Bible breathed from the lips of God so we can have the best of everything and live life the way we choose to live it? Is the Bible inspired so we can be a jet setter, a superstar, or a sports hero? No, no, and no!

Sometimes we forget verse 17, and it is the zinger in this passage: The Bible is inspired so the man or woman of God may be adequate, equipped for every good work. God has given us His wonderful Book so we will live for God, obey God, and do righteous works. We must carry on the work that Jesus left for us to do while there still is time. "We must work the works of Him who sent Me as long as it is day; night is coming when no one can work" (John 9:4).

Christians are made to do good works, according to this marvelous passage.

For we are His workmanship, created in Christ Jesus for good works, which God prepared beforehand so that we would walk in them.

—Ephesians 2:10

Let your mind dwell on the fact that we are God's workmanship, His handiwork. Think of the talents the Lord gave you, and then start listing all you can do for Him! Keep in mind the old sign: *God Doesn't Make Any Junk!*

JESUS WORKED

Look at the example Jesus left for us: "You know of Jesus of Nazareth, how God anointed Him with the Holy Spirit and with power, and how He went about doing good" (Acts 10:38).

We seem to forget what a hard worker Christ was. He was focused on the mission set before Him. He knew saving us was worth it all; He faced that huge task every day! There were people to be healed, souls to be taught, and defenses to be made to the daily traps set by the hypocrites. There were cities to be visited, territories to be covered, and the incessant demands of the throngs, not to mention the constant teaching, teaching, teaching.

> Jesus was going throughout all Galilee, teaching in their synagogues and proclaiming the gospel of the kingdom, and healing every kind of disease and every kind of sickness among the people. The news about Him spread throughout all Syria; and they brought to Him all who were ill, those suffering with various diseases and pains, demoniacs, epileptics, paralytics; and He healed them (Matthew 4:23–24).

> Many followed Him, and He healed them all (Matthew 12:15).

Jesus must have often been exhausted. And yet He never gave up and said, *I think that is enough! I need a vacation!* He simply went about doing good. Jesus had much work to do, and so do we. I have always thought how wonderful it would be if the world could say the very same thing about all Christians—we go about doing good.

Some say, "I'm a Christian." Others never say it, but you just know they are.

GOD WANTS A BIG FAMILY

God has given us His Word for many reasons. God wants us to know Him and His Son and the Holy Spirit.

- He has given us sixty-six books of history, prophecy, poetry, the gospel accounts, and epistles to teach us about who He is, who we are, and what He wants from us.
- The Bible tells us the story of Jesus, the Son of God, His saving gospel, and His death, burial, and resurrection—from the Old Testament to the New Testament.
- The Scriptures bring us comfort. They teach us of God's unfailing love and His desire for a relationship with us.
- The Bible teaches us about the unfathomable grace of God and His gift, the church.

Our Father inspired men to write His words for us so we can correct our wrongs and be saved. God has work for us to do while we are here, and the Word equips us in every way to accomplish those tasks. And let us never forget that the Word reveals the nature of God, His holiness and righteousness, and instructs the reader how to become God's child and look like Him. Most important, God has given us His Word to proclaim to a lost world. Mom used to say, "God wants a big family."

IT'S FOR ME!

Paul, inspired by the Holy Spirit, told the church in Rome: "For whatever was written in earlier times was written for our instruction, so that through perseverance and the encouragement of the Scriptures we might have hope" (Romans 15:4).

What was written in earlier times for the Roman church and all churches in the first century? The Old Testament. What did the accounts and stories of the old covenant do for the church then and the church now? They encouraged the church then and now, and the accounts give us all hope. What kind of hope? The hope of God's continual love, forgiveness, and salvation for every man. Let's not neglect whatever was written in earlier times! Those Scriptures encourage us to persevere and to have hope in the Lord.

It is also interesting to note that the Trinity—the Father, the Son, and the Holy Spirit—has made known to us God's will in the Scripture, the Holy Bible.

> But know this first of all, that no prophecy of Scripture is a matter of one's own interpretation, for no prophecy was ever made by an act of human will, but men moved by the Holy Spirit spoke from God (2 Peter 1:20–21).

> God, after He spoke long ago to the fathers in the prophets in many portions and in many ways, in these last days has spoken to us in His Son, whom He appointed heir of all things, through whom also He made the world (Hebrews 1:1–2).

Here is one of the very first scriptures I learned as a child, in two versions:

> Study to shew thyself approved unto God, a workman that needeth not to be ashamed, rightly dividing the word of truth (2 Timothy 2:15 KJV).

> Be diligent to present yourself approved to God as a workman who does not need to be ashamed, accurately handling the word of truth (2 Timothy 2:15 NASB).

For years I didn't see the key word *workman* here: a man or woman who works. It takes a lot of *work* to focus on God's Word. It takes a lot of *work* to do the will of God. It takes a lot of *work* and time to dig, research, and examine God's written Word. A friend of mine once said, "No matter how talented you are, it still takes work!" But think about this, girls. It takes a *decision* to work! I truly believe that laziness and selfishness keep the average Christian from achieving the potential God has in mind for her.

LIFE OR DEATH

In his marvelous book, *Muscle and a Shovel,* Michael Shank describes his arduous search for the truth:

> It took months of diligent digging. Tenacious and consistent digging into the Bible. Choosing to invest time into God's Word rather than to spend time doing the normal things that I did. It took muscle and a shovel.
>
> Muscle and a shovel to dig down beyond the mud and the sand and the gravel of a lifetime of erroneous religious teachings. I had to dig down beyond the denominational creeds, the religious confusion, the unbiblical practices, and all of the doctrines that opposed the New Testament's plain and simple Truth (318).

You see, Michael is a Pearl Seeker. He had to make the decision to dig for the truth on his own and all by himself. When he dug deeply into that wonderful treasure chest called the Bible, he discovered that the truth was there all along. Michael had never plunged himself into the depths of God's Word. He had allowed his mind to be covered with all kinds of religious error. Oh, how careful we must be with the Word of God, handling it and discerning it correctly! If the admonition from God is to handle the Word *accurately*, then we definitely can assume that it can be handled *inaccurately*. It is a matter of life and death—spiritual life and spiritual death—heaven and hell.

I remember an occasion when my elderly parents received a letter from a dear widow. She and her husband and my parents had spent many vacations together, and our families were often joined through the years. We all had done mission work, and as you can imagine, the topic of most conversations was centered on God. That widow made this interesting statement in her letter: "I just wish I could tell the teachers and preachers—where I live now and attend church—to tell me *what* the Bible says. Please don't tell me what you *think* it says."

I have inherited Your testimonies forever, for they are the joy of my heart. I have inclined my heart to perform Your statutes forever, even to the end.
—Psalm 119:111–112

HEARTBEAT OF THE EXEGETE

An exegete is one who works at understanding the Scripture, one who "draws out" its meaning. When we work at the Scriptures—when we study hard and take the Word apart verse by verse, word by word—then we realize that the Bible really is vibrantly alive and absolutely, unequivocally thrilling! Do we make the Bible come alive, or do we discover that the Bible is alive? There is nothing like discovering a hidden treasure in Scripture.

Perhaps you are assigned the story of David and Goliath to teach from the Bible, and perhaps you have read this passage a thousand times. Suddenly you observe a word or idea or thought you had never noticed. You sit up in amazement and study the passage again. You work at strengthening your understanding of the passage. Your heart soars, and before you know it, you have climbed up to the next rung on your ladder of spiritual maturity. I call this the heartbeat of the exegete. It doesn't end there, you know, for you cannot wait to share your new discovery with others. This is all in God's plan for you. He knew it all along.

I like to think of the Bible as being a huge treasure chest, open and brimming over with shiny, splendid jewels. This treasure chest is bottomless, having no end to it. God describes His Word this way:

> For the word of God is living and active and sharper than any two-edged sword, and piercing as far as the division of soul and spirit, of both joints and marrow, and able to judge the thoughts and intentions of the heart (Hebrews 4:12).

God is not dead and neither is His Word! It is alive and well and so sharp that it changes our lives. Brother Marshall Keeble so often said about this passage: "It cuts a-comin' and a-goin'." It cuts the Bible class teacher and the Bible class student alike. The teacher and the student are both learners. One can never understand every concept the Bible holds, because God is the author and He is infinite.

How amazing His Word is! The Bible slices and stabs us as we study God's admonitions, commandments, and rules for righteous living and raising faithful families. How moved we are as we read again and again the creation account, along with the stirring stories of heroes such as Noah, Moses, Joseph, Rahab, Esther, and Stephen!

We gasp as we read the accounts of Dinah, Jephthah, Gideon, Ananias and Sapphira, Apollos, and the Ethiopian eunuch. We grieve over an idolatrous and faithless Israel who continually played the harlot, turned her back on a forgiving God, and defiantly said to Him, "I reject You!" We stand at the old rugged cross and see our sweet Savior covered in His blood and our sins, paying a debt He did not owe. Then we look inward at our own lives, and our hearts are deeply wounded when we realize our own mammoth shortcomings and God's relatively small expectations of us.

HE'S STILL WORKING ON ME

However, God's Book reveals that God is not through with us yet. The God of the Bible is a God of love and forgiveness from the very first verse until the very last verse. From Genesis to Revelation we find hope, peace, and salvation all wrapped up in our wonderful Savior's forgiving love. And that is only the beginning.

I picture myself taking this two-edged sword and being able to plunge it into that magnificent treasure chest and go deeper and deeper. There is so much to be grasped that, with each stab and twist of this marvelous sword, I make several discoveries: God is in charge of all things; there are lessons to be learned; there are commandments to be obeyed; but most of all, there is Yahweh—our Jehovah God who must and will be heard.

If you are using this book as a part of a study group or a Bible class, here are some additional thoughts:

- Pray before and after your class time.
- Read every Scripture in every chapter.
- There is power in the Word of God.

- *Dunamis* (dynamite) is the Greek word for power.
- The Word is dynamite.

The Bible has the power to blow up our preconceived notions, to change our lives completely and at the same time restore our souls. Listen to how David describes the Word:

> The law of the Lord is perfect, restoring the soul; the testimony of the Lord is sure, making wise the simple. The precepts of the Lord are right, rejoicing the heart; the commandment of the Lord is pure, enlightening the eyes. The fear of the Lord is clean, enduring forever; the judgments of the Lord are true; they are righteous altogether. They are more desirable than gold, yes, than much fine gold; sweeter also than honey and the drippings of the honeycomb. Moreover, by them Your servant is warned; in keeping them there is great reward (Psalm 19:7–11).

STOP, LOOK, AND LISTEN!

You women who are studying together are traveling companions, taking a spiritual journey together. How blessed you are to have one another! Don't rush this book. Take rest stops along the way to pause, reflect, and discuss. Stop and pray and love one another. The Lord has much to tell us, teach us, and reveal to us. He knows those who seek His face and those who do not. What blessings you will receive as you open His Book and find the hidden gems! "He who gives attention to the word will find good, and blessed is he who trusts in the Lord" (Proverbs 16:20).

Let's reflect on Coffman's comments on this passage: "These clauses are parallel. The man that heeds the Word of God is exactly the same man that trusts in Jehovah. A man can do neither without doing both."

Oh, girls, the lesson is so simple and plain. When we stop, heed, and pay attention to the Word of God, then we find what is good. When we learn about God, we learn to trust Him and that makes us the happiest people on earth! Oh, that everyone would learn that!

Our world is in constant pursuit of happiness. The word *blessed* in the Bible is said to also mean happy. Listen to what David, the shepherd king

You shall walk in all the way which the Lord your God has commanded you, that you may live and that it may be well with you, and that you may prolong your days. . . .
—Deuteronomy 5:33

Find at least three other scriptures with the phrase "that it may be well with you." What are the implications?

of Israel, had to say about being happy: "How blessed are those whose way is blameless, who walk in the law of the Lord. How blessed are those who observe His testimonies, who seek Him with all their heart (Psalm 119:1–2).

In other words, happy are those who walk in the law of God, who obey His commandments, and who seek Him completely. Isn't this the true definition of a Pearl Seeker?

CHEATING WON'T WORK WITH GOD

I have the very first Bible my parents gave me the year I was baptized. Mom always inscribed a message when she gave the gift of a book, and my Bible was no different. She simply wrote this in my Bible: "This Book will keep you from sin, and sin will keep you from this Book."

In her book *Precious Are God's Plans*, Mom wrote:

> When I was a child, we occasionally had books in school that included the answers to questions asked or problems to be solved. These answers were in the back of the book.
>
> God gives us a detailed answer book. He entreats us, begs us, to look to Him for a happy and abundant life. He wants us to have wisdom, to know how to direct our daily lives, to have a good marriage, faithful children, a loving husband, peace of mind, and finally how to get home to Him.

Often we want a quick answer with little study. We even want to copy another's paper. We want to pass the test and have all the blessings with as little involvement as possible. And that's impossible. We want to look in the back of the book. We gain a little head knowledge but not a lot of heart knowledge. As I heard someone say, "We want to live like the rich man and die like Lazarus."

We have our answer book in our hands. What can be done to make us love it, study it, and meditate upon it? Who can persuade us to take the gift of His word into our hearts? (Fowler 119).

GOD IS LOOKING FOR ME

Remember, my sisters and friends, it is completely up to us whether or not we read our Bibles. God never forces anyone. The Bible can become our very best friend, alive and taken with us everywhere, or it can become a dust collector on our coffee table—just another book—never used and rotting away. This is our decision to make. No one can make it for us. God knows everything; He knows us. "The Lord has looked down from heaven upon the sons of men to see if there are any who understand, who seek after God" (Psalm 14:2).

It is also up to us to learn, grow, change, and be saved. Trust me on this one thought: Satan will work overtime to do everything he possibly can to keep you out of God's marvelous Word! He wants to keep you and me as illiterate, uneducated, and stupid as possible. Someone has said that the devil's most powerful tool is man's ignorance of God's Word! Don't let Satan win! Be strong. The Lord will help you. He is bigger than Satan! "You are from God, little children, and have overcome them; because greater is He who is in you than he who is in the world" (1 John 4:4).

Is there ever a time when we stop seeking the Lord and His will for us? Is there a time when we know enough? No! We can never know everything there is to know. Look at Paul's admonition to the church at Colossae: "If then you have been raised up with Christ, keep seeking the things above, where Christ is, seated at the right hand of God" (Colossians 3:1).

Keep seeking, keep asking questions, keep on learning.

GOD'S BLESSINGS ON THE SEEKER

Here is one more precious passage on seeking the Lord—a passage with a promise from God. "The Lord is good to those who wait for Him, to the person who seeks Him" (Lamentations 3:25). Oh, yes, the Lord is good to the seeker—the Pearl Seeker. There are blessings just waiting for us!

The voice of a young boy named Samuel echoes across the pages of the Bible. God called him by name, and unafraid, he answered his Master's call: "Speak, for Your servant is listening" (1 Samuel 3:10). When we read and study God's Word, we hear God calling our name, too. Will we, too, answer the Master, "Speak, for Your servant is listening"?

It is so true, my precious sisters, that we make the decision of how spiritual we will be. We make the choice to seek God—He never forces us. We make the choice to cherish the Pearl or throw it away.

Prayer: Lord, help me to be a Pearl Seeker. Help me to seek You and Your strength. Help me to seek Your face continually.

Song: Ancient Words

Holy words long preserved
For our walk in this world;
They resound with God's own heart,
Oh, let the ancient words impart.

Chorus:
Ancient words ever true
Changing me and changing you;
We have come with open hearts,
Oh, let the ancient words impart.

Words of Life, words of Hope
Give us strength, help us cope
In this world, where e'er we roam,
Ancient words will guide us home.

Holy words of our Faith,
Handed down to this age,
Came to us through sacrifice,
Oh heed the faithful words of Christ.

Holy words long preserved
For our walk in this world;
They resound with God's own heart
Oh let the ancient words impart

—Ronnie C. Freeman, Jr /
Tony W. Wood, Lyrics

Digging for Pearls

1. What are some ideas to make Bible study clearer and more meaningful?

2. Read Psalm 119 and discuss the passages that describe the Word of God and its power.

3. If we are happy when we delight in the Bible, read the Bible, and meditate on its powerful words, what will be the result in our lives? (Refer to the following page.)

- Write Psalm 1:1–3 below to find obvious results.

- How does this passage define real happiness?

- Those who walk in the law of God, obey His commandments, seek Him completely, delight in His law, and meditate on it constantly . . . How is this the true definition of a Pearl Seeker?

4. Choose four words that describe God at work in the following verse: "Is not My word like fire?" declares the Lord, "and like a hammer which shatters a rock?" (Jeremiah 23:29).

Weak	Dynamite	Outdated	Power
Ineffective	Fire	Hammer	Volatile

Pearl Drop

I Gotta Be Me!

How many of you have ever seen that famous picture of three owls sitting on a tree limb? Two of the owls are doing what all the owls should be doing: sitting there, eyes straight ahead, just being good little owls. But the third owl is hanging upside down, swinging back and forth, and facing backwards.

I, my friends, am that third owl, or at least I was at one time. I was and still am, to a certain extent, a different thinker. I have always been strong-willed—okay, stubborn—determined to have my own way. I have always questioned the rules, why they had to be totally opposite of what I wanted. I was the youngest of the family, the baby, and I enjoyed every minute of it, except when it came to rules. Just ask my brother Tom. "Why can't I go outside?" "Why can't I buy that outfit?" "Why do I have to clean the church building?" "Why can't I stay out late?" And on and on it went.

Mom nicknamed me Caledonia, after some song she knew from the dark ages about a hard-headed girl. She used to sing it to me: "Caledonia, Caledonia, what makes your big head so hard?" I would tell her my theme song was Sammy Davis Jr.'s "I Gotta Be Me," and sing it right back to her.

When I was age nine, our family went to New England on a summer vacation. I did not realize it at the time, but my parents were contemplating moving there to do mission work. We traveled to Boston, a huge, bustling city, the biggest one I had ever seen! Part of our excursion consisted of traveling on the MTA, Boston's underground transit system. According to the Kingston Trio, that is where Charlie got lost and never returned!

As I stood on the platform staring at the enormous trains and wondering at all the loud noises, I noticed gigantic signs: "Don't spit on the tracks!" I walked over to my mother and said, "I can't help it. I gotta spit!" She laughed so hard she almost fell off the platform and onto the rails! That which was forbidden was the very thing I wanted to do. I always wanted to please my parents, but I was like a lot of kids: I was immature and made some stupid decisions.

Why Do You Fight Me?

Years ago there was a book written on the birth order of children and their types of personalities. The author pointed out that the youngest of the family—the baby—lives with one theme continually running in her head: "The rules do not apply." This described me to a "T." Even if I had been forbidden to do so and so, I stepped over the line of obedience and defied my parents and God. I broke many rules and refused to conform. I can remember countless "discipline" sessions with Mom's hairbrush or paddle or spatula—she just grabbed whatever was handy at the moment—as she believed she was in charge! Can you imagine such a thing? How often I remember my mother saying to me, "Becky, why do you fight me? Why won't you just do what I say?"

I thank God that He loved me in spite of my willfulness. I thank God that my parents loved me in spite of my willfulness. I fought Him and I fought my parents and I fought myself and I was miserable. I knew better. I knew the right thing to do, but I didn't want to do it. I wanted my way. I, I, I. Underneath—in my heart of hearts—I wanted to do better. But I just was not ready to change.

Living my life that way was no fun. Immaturity is a "hard row to hoe." I was at odds with my parents and the Lord. That's no way to live, my friends. It is life at the bottom of the barrel. But the Lord never stopped loving me nor did He give up on me. He let me live through a tough summer, constantly showing me His way was superior to anything else on this planet. I went through a very taxing year at college, feeling all alone and like a fish out of water. But the Lord was teaching me many lessons, and He took His time.

Goodbye, Miss Caledonia

Finally, I woke up, grew up, and got the message. Miss Caledonia became Sweet Becky. I wanted to do things His way. I wanted to please Him, and I finally surrendered my will to His. My heart, life, strength, soul, and mind were His, and everything changed. God met me where I was and took me where I needed to be. My life went from "no life" to "abundant life." I became a Pearl Seeker.

Life on that tree branch is fabulous now for this third owl. I am not upside down and swinging backwards, but I am cooperating and behaving. That does not mean I cannot be a free thinker and ask my "why?" questions. I have a very inquisitive mind! But I have changed. I have *chosen* to serve God. He is number one in my life, and I have made the decision to please Him. I have made the decision to follow Him and obey what He says. I never fight Him. I have learned I can't overcome God. He always wins, and I always lose. Life with the Lord is so much better than life with Satan, whom I had chosen unintentionally. I want to be the Lord's friend, not His enemy.

For those of you who are "third owls," let me say one more thing. There is nothing wrong with being a free spirit or free thinker or marching to the beat of a different drummer. Nothing at all. However, it becomes wrong in my book when the owl rejects God—plain and simple. Oh, I can still sing, "I gotta be me . . ." and delight in the DNA that God has given me. But now if my way conflicts with His way, I choose His way every time, even when I do not understand. I finally grew up, got the picture, and realized that God has a plan for me (Jeremiah 29:11–13), and His plan is glorious! I also have found this to be true: Eventually the third owl must flip back up on that tree branch and cooperate with the Lord, or she will find herself living a life filled with great sorrow, conflict, and ulcers. There will be no peace.

The glorious thing that I have learned? I have learned that this is the life He has chosen for me. What a shame it would have been to have missed out on it! Here I am just as happy as I can be—and at peace. Why? Because I am pleasing Him, and that's all that counts. *God's way is the best way to live.* Do I have a perfect life? Of course not! Who does? Are there problems and crises? All the time. But, you see, God is in charge. He has my back, and I surrender all. What could be more wonderful? Obedience brings real happiness.

It is important to me to be real, straight, and sincere, so I have been very "gut honest" with you, my sisters. I just want to help you. June Carter was known to say many times, "I'm just tryin' to matter." Well, girls, I'm just tryin' to matter, too!

I thought you would like to know that Mom stopped calling me Caledonia, and the Lord started calling me His servant, His daughter, His girl, His owl, and His little sparrow.

CHAPTER 2

Seek The Lord's Pleasure

For the Lord takes pleasure in His people; He will beautify the afflicted ones with salvation (Psalm 149:4).

Finally then, brethren, we request and exhort you in the Lord Jesus, that as you received from us instruction as to how you ought to walk and please God (just as you actually do walk), that you excel still more (1 Thessalonians 4:1).

One of the aspects of Bible reading that I love the most is discovering a passage that seems to jump off the page at me. It may be only a verse or several words, but often a passage startles me, hits me right between the eyes, and makes me stop and think! I just love it when that happens! Many times, the excerpt helps me to grow and understand further my identity as a Christian woman, and it becomes a part of my life from that moment on.

One such selection is Ephesians 5:6–10. Here the Holy Spirit inspired the apostle Paul to write encouraging words to the Ephesian Christians long ago and to us today as we walk the walk:

> Let no one deceive you with empty words, for because of these things the wrath of God comes upon the sons of disobedience. Therefore do not be partakers with them; for you were formerly darkness, but now you are Light in the Lord; walk as children of Light (for the fruit of the Light consists in all goodness and righteousness and truth), trying to learn what is pleasing to the Lord (Ephesians 5:6–10).

Before obeying the gospel of Jesus, we were children of darkness. We did not walk in the Light because we were not obedient to Jesus who is the Light. But our hearts were touched as we heard the gospel message, and everything changed. We believed, we repented of our sins, we confessed that Jesus is the Son of God, and we were buried with Him in baptism. We became children of God, disciples of Christ, followers, children of the King—Christians. We're new creatures, no longer seeking to do things our way but rather seeking to please the Lord.

GREAT CHANGES

Listen to how Jesus described Himself in John 8:12: "I am the Light of the world; he who follows Me will not walk in the darkness, but will have the Light of life." Jesus further said, "I am the way, and the truth, and the life; no one comes to the Father but through Me" (John 14:6).

When we walk as children of Light, we come to know Christ, and we begin to make some very important changes in our lifestyle. In fact, our whole life changes.

- We begin to realize that we are in the world but not of the world.
- We make better friends, because we cannot be with our old crowd that delighted in immoral living.
- We change the way we talk because we now watch our vocabulary, our behavior, and our actions.
- We don't dress the way we used to, because we want to look like a Christian and not like the world.
- We are obedient to God's commandments, and our focus is now on Him and not on ourselves.
- We become more consistent in our church attendance, because we love our spiritual family and garner strength from them.
- We grow in our love for God's Word, and we want to share it with others.

- We discover that the truth of the gospel is so compelling that we cannot let it go! Our missionary friend Hulen Masters once said, "You cannot hear the truth and be the same again!"

All of these things take time. A lifetime. We make many mistakes, but we truly rejoice because there is forgiveness now. We belong to Jesus and are in constant contact with His blood (1 John 1:7).

LEARNING TO PLEASE

It is verse 10 of Ephesians 5 that I call my zinger verse: ". . . trying to learn what is pleasing to the Lord." This verse made me catch my breath. Girls, I want to please God; I want to please Jesus; I want to please the Holy Spirit—the three Beings that comprise the Trinity. It's that simple. This verse speaks to me as a Christian and as a woman, for this is my quest: to please God. That is when I am happiest.

Now I must be honest and tell you that I have not always chosen to live for the Lord and obey His commandments. Like Frank Sinatra's theme song, I desired to do everything "my way." But I had to grow up, and the Lord was patient and merciful. I am thankful to Him for loving me like this. Tell me, hasn't the Lord been merciful with you? Has He forgiven you?

It is human nature to want to be happy and to please those around us. Do we actually want to alienate our loved ones or the Lord? Not many of us do.

Jim Sheerer had this to say about Ephesians 5:6–10 in his *New Testament Commentary:*

> As a Christian does what God commands him to do, he will bear the fruit of the light. This will prove he is pleasing unto the Lord. The intense desire of the Christian is to be pleasing unto God (835).

What must I do to begin to please God? I must get into the Word! I must read His book and see what He has to say about Himself and what He wants of men and women. I must open His Book and read, study, and meditate.

WHAT ARE YOU DOING? AND THINKING?

Remember: Satan will do everything he possibly can to keep you from opening a Bible! He does not want you in the Word at all! He hates God and he hates His Word. Satan will make you too busy to read or study; he will fill your daily life with so many irrelevant things and will keep you too tired for anything spiritual. All you will want to do is sleep. Reading the Bible and praying are the furthest things from your mind when you are tired. And Satan wants every Bible closed shut!

An important scripture comes to mind even now:

> Finally, brethren, whatever is true, whatever is honorable, whatever is right, whatever is pure, whatever is lovely, whatever is of good repute, if there is any excellence and if anything worthy of praise, let your mind dwell on these things (Philippians 4:8).

What does "let your mind dwell" really mean? It means to ponder, to meditate, to consider. A good Bible student cannot rush through the Bible grabbing thoughts at random and then hope to mature in the faith and please God. (That is merely cafeteria-style learning.) Acquiring knowledge of His Word takes time, effort, and a willing heart. *It is a daily commitment to time alone with the Father.* It is learning the whole truth and nothing but the truth! Surely that kind of study pleases the Father.

DO YOU KNOW YOUR FATHER?

Put yourself in God's shoes (if He wears shoes). How do you feel when your own children—grown up or not—come to you and genuinely want to know more about you: your childhood, your decision to become a Christian, and such like? You are delighted! It thrills you that your child wants to know more about you and wants to spend time with you—just with you. And you want to love that child all the more. You even want to do special things for him or her. Ah, now you get the picture. What an amazing correlation there is in the love and blessings we have for our children and the love and blessings God has for His children as they seek to know Him better.

There are all kinds of gifts waiting for us as we strive to learn more about our Father: "See how great a love the Father has bestowed on us, that we should be called children of God; and such we are. For this reason the world does not know us, because it did not know Him" (1 John 3:1).

The world does not know God nor does it desire to know God. The world cares only about the world. The apostle John was inspired to write these words to Christians to assure them that God calls them His children.

What a blessing! If you are a Christian, you are His child. As God's child, you want to know more about your Father: who He is and what He wants of you. Whether in the first century with the apostles or the last century yet to come, God answers every question and even describes His infinite love through the Bible, His revealed Word. Why? Because God wants His children to know Him.

GOD KNOWS ME

Here is one of the most fascinating scriptures in the entire Bible:

> Thus says the Lord, "Let not a wise man boast of his wisdom, and let not the mighty man boast of his might, let not a rich man boast of his riches; but let him who boasts boast of this, that he understands and knows Me, that I am the Lord" (Jeremiah 9:23–24).

In modern day language, God says, "Don't brag about your brains, brawn, or your dollar bills. If you are going to brag about anything, then brag that you know and understand Me!"

If I am going to know and understand God, I must first find Him in His Word. The Bible is God's story of His love for mankind. It is difficult for me to understand the marvelous love of my God. Why does God love me so much? Why does the Father love all of us so much? Is this difficult for you? I know what I am—deep down. And so does God. I know Becky through and through. And so does God. I live with Becky every moment and every second of the day, and there is no way that I can fool God. But in spite of all this, He still loves me and forgives me.

"But You know me, O Lord; You see me; and You examine my heart's attitude toward You" (Jeremiah 12:3). He is the God of second chances and third chances and on and on.

When I become depressed or am feeling unloved or all alone, I think of a little sparrow and rely on Jesus' words for comfort:

> Are not two sparrows sold for a cent? And yet not one of them will fall to the ground apart from your Father. But the very hairs of your head are all numbered. So do not fear; you are more valuable than many sparrows (Matthew 10:29–31).

I remind myself that I am one loved little sparrow. My Father knows when I am troubled, when I am hurt, and when I fall to the ground. He knows when my heart is torn in two. He knows my fear, knows my heartaches, and fixes me! And passages like this one in Matthew 10 truly make me love my Father more. And when I love God, I want to please God. And nothing else matters. Nothing.

God knows you through and through. He loves you no matter what. I know that He has forgiven you time after time, hasn't He? But hear me on this: Satan will do everything in his power to keep you and me from having any knowledge of our Father's love for us. Are you beginning to understand now why Satan works overtime to keep us from reading the Bible? He will go to great lengths to stop church attendance, commitment, faithfulness, and true "agape" love in our lives.

THE CROSS IS PERSONAL

Come with me to Calvary and stand at the foot of that old rugged cross. Let's look upon Jesus' face and see the love looking right back at us. When we see the blood shed for our own sins, we begin to know what it means to love the Lord, to really love the Lord. And perhaps we can understand 1 John 4:19 just a little more when it says, "We love, because He first loved us." And then we begin to grasp the passage we hold so dear to our hearts: "For God so loved the world, that He gave His only begotten Son, that whoever believes in Him should not perish, but have eternal life (John 3:16).

Two preacher quotes come to my mind. The first is by Matt Phillips from California, and the other is by Flavil Nichols from Alabama.

1. *If we are not bearing fruit for God, we don't really understand what God has done for us!* In other words, if we are not doing good works for the Lord, we are not honestly looking at our own sinful lives or the sacrifice of the Lamb of God for us. We don't see the blood; we don't see the stripes; we don't see the crown of thorns. We don't want to really look at the cross, do we? Because if we really stood and looked at our suffering Savior, our hearts might be touched and then we would have to do something in return. We just will not allow that to happen!

2. *When Jesus died for me, He made it personal!* Jesus' sacrificing Himself on that Roman cross is serious business, my sister. And He did it all for you and for me. He could have called ten thousand angels, but He died alone for you and me.

Why doesn't everyone love God? Why doesn't everyone want to be a Christian? Why doesn't every Christian want to be a Pearl Seeker? Why doesn't everyone want to please the Lord? I will never understand why. The Master of the universe holds His mighty arms out to us to bless us, save us, love us, and call us His own, and many reject everything about Him and walk away. How foolish! Why would anyone play Russian roulette with his soul and eternity?

NOT ABOUT ME?

My friends, pleasing God means first of all that our own self has been killed, and the focus has shifted from ourselves to Him. Look at what Paul wrote: "I have been crucified with Christ; and it is no longer I who live, but Christ lives in me" (Galatians 2:20). He also told the Corinthians, "I protest, brethren, by the boasting in you, which I have in Christ Jesus our Lord, I die daily" (1 Corinthians 15:31).

Pleasing the Father means that no longer are we submerged in our own wants and needs, but now our whole world revolves around what

God needs from us. It means that we have learned that it is all about God and not about us. It means that we are now a living sacrifice—not a dead one. "I urge you, brethren, by the mercies of God, to present your bodies a living and holy sacrifice, acceptable to God, which is your spiritual service of worship" (Romans 12:1).

Pleasing God means surrender. It means selflessness. It means that He is number one! It is consciously and conscientiously making the magnificent decision to climb up on that altar and die every single day that we live this Christian life! And that is not easy for selfish mankind or selfish Christians. A preacher once said, "The fear of the Lord is the overwhelming desire to do nothing to displease God!"

SURRENDER AND WALK WITH GOD

My sisters, I am here to tell you—with all the love in my heart—that when you choose to love our precious Father, His Son, and His Spirit, you have chosen what is good and right and true—righteousness. And when you choose to surrender to His will and no longer to yourself, you are choosing to please Him. That is what Pearl Seekers do. And when you choose God, you will find that you are among the most blessed women on the face of this earth! Let me tell you what happens when you completely give it up—when you completely yield to His will for you. God will wrap you in His arms. Where else would you rather be?

Do you remember anything about the man Enoch? Let's challenge ourselves right now to see and learn what the Lord has to say about him.

> Enoch lived sixty-five years, and became the father of Methuselah. Then Enoch walked with God three hundred years after he became the father of Methuselah, and he had other sons and daughters. So all the days of Enoch were three hundred and sixty-five years. And Enoch walked with God; and he was not, for God took him (Genesis 5:21–24).

From these verses we see that Enoch had a relationship with God. He walked with Him; they were friends and companions. Was Enoch the first man with whom God ever walked? No, we are told in Genesis 6:9, "Noah was a righteous man, blameless in his time; Noah walked with God." And remember that Adam and Eve hid themselves when they heard the sound of God's walking in the garden (Genesis 3:8). They knew the sound of God's walk.

Walking together denotes a friendship, a time for talking and becoming acquainted. Walking together describes the birth and strengthening of a relationship. What was it like for Adam and Eve to walk with God? Don't you wonder? I surely do. However, it is interesting to note that we are never told in the Bible that God walked with immoral people or rebellious people.

LET'S BE PLEASING TO GOD

It seems to me that we all want a relationship with our God. Someone has said that we are all trying to get back to Eden. We want what Adam and Eve had in that garden so long ago. It does make sense.

The Bible tells us that Enoch walked with God, so he and God evidently had a friendship. And that friendship must have been very special because the rest of the verse tells us that God took Enoch. Took him where? Took him away from this earth to avoid experiencing death. Enoch did not die a physical death as everyone else has done or will do, that is, everyone except those alive at the Lord's return. God took him ahead of time.

Enoch was surrounded by ancestors who lived hundreds of years. His son Methuselah lived longer than any other man of whom we have a record, 969 years. But Enoch lived only 365 years.

But let's not stop here; let's move to the New Testament and notice a very important attribute of Enoch: "By faith Enoch was taken up so that he would not see death; and he was not found because God took him up; for he obtained the witness that before his being taken up he was pleasing to God" (Hebrews 11:5).

The Hebrews writer reveals how God felt about Enoch. He was so pleased with Enoch that He took him rather than let him die. God is omniscient—He knows all things. God knew Enoch's heart, and He knew that Enoch wanted to please Him. Notice that God, not the angels, took Enoch. God did it Himself.

Do you want to please God? Do I want to please God? He knows our hearts. Trying to learn what is pleasing to the Lord should be the desire of every single Christian. That desire describes my life right now. It is my passion. How do I keep that fire burning? I must sit at my Master's feet and keep asking my Father questions about Himself. I must read His story as He has recorded it. I must learn from it and do those things that please Him. I must put to death the old person described in Romans 6:6, as Paul did. I call it killing the old girl. I must grow my faith. Hasn't He already told us how to obtain faith in the first place? "So faith comes from hearing, and hearing by the word of Christ" (Romans 10:17).

Immediately following the description of Enoch's pleasing God, the following verse elaborates: "And without faith it is impossible to please Him, for he who comes to God must believe that He is, and that He is a rewarder of those who seek Him" (Hebrews 11:6).

That is the formula for pleasing our Jehovah God! If we are going to come to God, then we must believe in Him and believe that He is the one in charge, the Rewarder, the trophy giver to those who seek His face. Remember, not all people desire to seek God. Mom would often say, "There are many people who believe in God but don't believe God." How true.

PLEASING GOD IS WORK

Many people say, "I want Jesus to be my personal Savior," but they do not want Him to be the Lord of their lives. That would mean they would have to surrender to Him, and they are not willing to do that. In America, millions believe there is a God, but they don't believe what He says in His Book, and they surely don't want to have to work or obey Him. There are also millions who believe that all one has to do is believe there is a God, and that is enough for salvation.

The King James Version supplies the word *diligently* in front of the word *seek* in Hebrews 11:6, not because it appears in the original text but because the idea of diligence is inherent in the Greek word translated *seek*. A nineteenth century British theologian had this to say about the word *seek*: "Wherever it occurs in the New Testament in the sense of searching, it suggests the notion of strenuous endeavor" (Westcott 356).

There it is again: The aspect of hard work, the workman we talked about in chapter 1, the Pearl Seeker. Mr. Westcott was right: Seeking God is a strenuous endeavor. It takes hard work to turn off the TV, shut down the computer, open the Bible, and learn. It takes discipline on our part! We have to learn to be quiet and let the Lord speak. After all, didn't He inspire these words to be written: "Be still, and know that I am God"? (Psalm 46:10 NKJV). My sisters, we have forgotten how to be still and be quiet.

FORMULA FOR HIS PLEASURE

In addition to Colossians 1:10–12 in the margin, a few more passages shed light on the concept of pleasing the Lord: "Therefore we also have as our ambition, whether at home or absent, to be pleasing to Him" (2 Corinthians 5:9). Also consider 1 Thessalonians 2:4: "But just as we have been approved by God to be entrusted with the gospel, so we speak, not as pleasing men, but God who examines our hearts."

As I write today, we are just barely into a new year and conversations still abound with thoughts and determinations, and some failures already, of New Year resolutions. It is a beginning-again of resolve in areas of our lives that need fixing.

WALK WITH HIM

My sister, how is your walk with God? Is your lifestyle pleasing to Him? Are you a

. . . so that you will walk in a manner worthy of the Lord, to please Him in all respects, bearing fruit in every good work and increasing in the knowledge of God; strengthened with all power, according to His glorious might, for the attaining of all steadfastness and patience; joyously giving thanks to the Father, who has qualified us to share in the inheritance of the saints in Light.

—Colossians 1:10–12

Make a list of specific actions you plan to take to "please Him in all respects."

____

____

____

____

____

____

____

daily Bible reader? Do you stop and pray every day? How important is He to you? Do you even want to please the Lord?

Recently I was working on some spiritual lessons in my office. For several weeks I had studied God's Word and delved deeply into His precious Book. I prayed constantly for guidance, wisdom, and understanding. I met God every morning and spent the entire day with Him—from dawn until dusk. Towards the end of this study period, I went into the kitchen for a moment, stepped over to the sink, and gazed out my kitchen window into God's beautiful creation. I felt such deep feelings of peace. I wondered why I felt this way, and it occurred to me, "Well, Becky, you have been walking with the Lord. You've been spending time with Him."

Oh girls, nothing feels better than spending time with the Lord! Why does it take us so long to figure this out?

In Nehemiah 8, God's people who came with Nehemiah to rebuild the walls of Jerusalem gathered in the open square in front of Jerusalem's Water Gate to celebrate their work and hear of God's plans for them. At their request, Ezra the scribe read the law of the Lord to them. When they discovered that the Feast of the Booths had not been observed properly, they determined that would never happen again. They quickly gathered tree branches and constructed booths on their housetops. This feast had been observed in the past but never celebrated this joyously!

> The entire assembly of those who had returned from the captivity made booths and lived in them. The sons of Israel had indeed not done so from the days of Joshua the son of Nun to that day. And there was great rejoicing (Nehemiah 8:17).

Look at the last sentence of this verse, "And there was great rejoicing." Why? Because the people obeyed God's commands, and obeying God brings happiness every time! The people had a heart for God and wanted to please Him.

If we took a church poll today and asked how many Christians want to please God, every hand would go up! But how many hands would go up if we took another poll and asked how many are daily Bible readers?

I think we would be absolutely shocked. What about prayer? How many Christians pray every day? The numbers are slim and nowhere near what they should be. How do we rate? Let's all take an honest look at the woman in the mirror:

> But prove yourselves doers of the word, and not merely hearers who delude themselves. For if anyone is a hearer of the word and not a doer, he is like a man who looks at his natural face in a mirror; for once he has looked at himself and gone away, he has immediately forgotten what kind of person he was. But one who looks intently at the perfect law, the law of liberty, and abides by it, not having become a forgetful hearer but an effectual doer, this man will be blessed in what he does (James 1:22–25).

To please God we must have faith in Him and obey Him. We must make time for God and take time for God every day. How can we possibly have faith or please the Lord if we never open His precious letters from Home? It just cannot happen.

ORDINARY MEN, EXTRAORDINARY GOD

- *Enoch.* He had faith, and he pleased the Lord. He pleased God so much that God scooped him up from his earthly home and personally escorted him to his eternal home. What a fabulous excursion Enoch got to take! I envy that.
- *Obedient Jews.* The Jews returning from captivity listened to the Law of the Lord day after day after day. They discovered a commandment that had not been completely observed for years, and their hearts were not content until they had put this commandment wholly back into their lives. As a result, the Bible tells us there was great rejoicing. Not just a little rejoicing—but great rejoicing (Nehemiah 8:17).
- *David.* Only David the shepherd king rated the following compliment from the Lord: "After He had removed him, He raised up David to be their king, concerning whom He also testified and said, 'I have found David the son of Jesse, a man after My heart, who will

do all My will'" (Acts 13:22). God does not designate anyone else as a person after His own heart—no one but David. But there is a zinger here. Look at the rest of the verse: ". . . who will do all my will." God loved David so very much because David pleased God by always doing what God wanted of him.

- *Abraham.* What does God say about Abraham that is not said about anyone else in the Bible? Listen to this accolade: "And the Scripture was fulfilled which says, 'And Abraham believed God, and it was reckoned to him as righteousness,' and he was called the friend of God" (James 2:23).

  Abraham received one of the highest compliments from Almighty God that any created human could ever receive! God called him His friend. Why did God do that? This scripture in James shows us that Abraham believed God and that it was reckoned to him as righteousness. Abraham acted on that faith! He proved his faith by his works.

  God called him from a faraway land and told him to get up and move! Move where? Wherever God told him to move! Read the Genesis 12 depiction of this stirring, faith-building, wondrous account where father Abraham showed his love and deep abiding faith in God by acting on God's command to leave Haran.

  When God tested Abraham's faith again, ten chapters later, Abraham still demonstrated his love for God by offering Isaac, the son of promise, as God had commanded. How do you lay your own precious son on a bed of sticks and proceed to draw your knife to slay him without believing that your God will deliver both of you? That takes a huge faith, doesn't it? But it's not impossible!

Enoch, David, and Abraham all pleased God. They were obedient sons of their heavenly Father, and God blessed all of them richly. Did these three have perfect lives? No, nobody gets that. But they were men who set the right example for us—even today as we live in our fast-paced society. They were ordinary men who loved and obeyed our extraordinary God! God had a huge plan for them, and they worked the plan.

We can do that, too. We can please God and walk with God and be the friend of God and have a heart like God, but first we must obey God. It is as simple as that.

THE WAY YOU SHOULD GO

I read a statement by E. Lewis from a past issue of Twenty-first Century Christian's *Power for Today* that has been a great help on my journey with the Lord: "Sometimes we feel we must do some great work to be successful in God's eyes, but God wants us first to do the work where we are!" God has placed us exactly where He wants us. David could easily say, "The lines have fallen to me in pleasant places; indeed, my heritage is beautiful to me" (Psalm 16:6). What are we doing for the Lord? Are we blooming where we are planted, or are we misery and negativity personified?

Faith is the first step in pleasing God, so how is your faith? Read His Book. Build your faith. Work the plan. Take it slowly, one step at a time, for He has much to say and much to teach you and me. Listen carefully as He assures David: "I will instruct you and teach you in the way which you should go" (Psalm 32:8). Does He love us any less? He further tells us: "If you love Me, you will keep My commandments" (John 14:15).

It is not too late to start, so let us begin again. Let's love again and let's love more from now on. May it be said of each of us: *She walked with God; she pleased God; she was a woman after God's own heart. She was a friend of God.*

"For I know the plans that I have for you," declares the Lord, "plans for welfare and not for calamity to give you a future and a hope. Then you will call upon Me and come and pray to Me, and I will listen to you. You will seek Me and find Me when you search for Me with all your heart."

—Jeremiah 29:11–13

Our kind Father has wonderful plans for you. How are you working that plan?

____

____

____

____

____

____

____

____

____

____

____

Prayer: Lord, help me to be pleasing to You.

Song: Have Thine Own Way, Lord

Have Thine own way, Lord! Have Thine own way!
Thou art the Potter, I am the clay.
Mold me and make me after Thy will,
While I am waiting, yielded and still.

Have Thine own way, Lord! Have Thine own way!
Search me and try me, Master, today!
Whiter than snow, Lord, wash me just now,
As in Thy presence humbly I bow.

Have Thine own way, Lord! Have Thine own way!
Wounded and weary, help me, I pray!
Power, all power, surely is Thine!
Touch me and heal me, Savior divine.

Have Thine own way, Lord! Have Thine own way!
Hold o'er my being absolute sway!
Fill with Thy Spirit 'till all shall see
Christ only, always, living in me.

Digging for Pearls

1. Why doesn't everyone love God?
2. If we want to please God, what are some actions we must take?
3. What did Abraham do that caused him to be called the friend of God?

Pearl Drop

The Kitchen Table

We called our home "Grand Central Station" because it was always filled with people coming and going. When I came home from school, there was usually a Bible class going on in the kitchen, or perhaps a new Christian family had dropped by for encouragement or advice. Many times there was a couple in the kitchen, a preacher and his wife, stopping by for a cup of coffee on their way home. Whoever was there, they were gathered at our favorite spot—the kitchen table.

When my brother Tom went off to college, one of his letters began this way, "Dear Mom, Dad, Judy, Becky, and whoever else just walked in the front door." Yes, that is exactly the way it was. Dad should have installed big revolving front doors in all our houses, for as one visitor left, another walked right in! That was our life in the mission field.

Mom was one terrific hostess. She was a "people person" with a exuberant sense of humor and a wonderful laugh, the kind that people gravitate toward. As a little girl when I got lost at church, all I ever did was stop and listen for her laugh. She was like Lucille Ball—just naturally funny. She genuinely liked people of all walks and ilks, and they liked her. She knew instinctively what people needed—food, talk, and the Lord. You could always count on a lively conversation of some kind happening at her table, along with a snack on which to nibble.

Mom was a wonderful listener and a very wise woman, ready to give her opinion when it was needed. She was also very frugal and an excellent cook. She had been a child of the Depression, raised by a thrifty Scottish father. Somehow she could feed a family of five on next to nothing! We knew that payday was near when supper consisted of pinto beans and cornbread—or salmon patties.

Now let me say something about those salmon cakes. I don't know how in the world Mom could open a can of salmon, add some magic ingredients, and somehow feed three hungry kids and two adults, but she did. That was and still is a true talent in my book.

Y'all Come Over

During my formative years, we lived next door to the church building in Concord, New Hampshire. People loved to visit us after worship. I can still see them lined up as we exited the church building, eagerly hoping for those wonderful words from Mama: "Y'all come on over to the house!" It just seemed normal to have anywhere from 4 to 104 guests congregating in our home.

The Bibles Were Opened

I remember, as a young girl growing up in the Fowler household, sitting on the floor at the entrance of the living room or kitchen, listening to the grown-ups and all their lively conversations. They told a lot of jokes, teased one another, and laughed incessantly. And I haven't even mentioned the gatherings around the piano! We had such fun singing "Autumn Leaves" and the score from *The Music Man,* and other popular songs of the day.

However, after the food was served and things calmed down a bit, someone would say, "I don't know if I understood the sermon tonight, Russ," or "What does that scripture really mean?" or "How do I teach the gospel where I work?" Invariably there was a scrambling for all the Bibles to be brought out, and like clockwork, the Bibles were opened, a study began, and God spoke through His Word to all of us gathered there.

I didn't understand all the questions and answers; I just knew I wanted to be in on it! I listened to various opinions and heartfelt questions that made me stop and think. The discussions around our table were profound and life-changing. It was Christianity at its best—an intense search for the Almighty. When the Bibles were opened, the quest of the Pearl Seeker came alive and beckoned to each soul gathered there! It was as if we felt God's calling each of us to a clearer understanding of His Word. This quest for God seemed to reach down into all of our souls and knock on the door of our hearts. I simply cannot find the words to describe it accurately.

Day-old Is Fine

Now some of you may ask, "Becky, how in the world did your mom feed all those people?" Great question! I told you how Mom was a thrifty food manager. When she went grocery shopping, she carried coupons and hit every store in town that had a special. On top of that, she adored day-old bakery stores. I begged her constantly, "Mom, can we please have a fresh loaf of bread this week?" And her consistent reply was, "No! It costs too much! Day-old is fine." I never won that round. She stocked up on old doughnuts, pastries—you name it. Then she froze all those delicacies in our huge, old Amana freezer.

When company came over, she would slap those old doughnuts on a cookie sheet, ramp the oven up to 500 degrees, and cook them as fast as possible. She burned the bottoms of them every single time. Trust me, I know these things. Laughing, she would scrape off what she could, put the odd looking things on a plate, mix up some hot chocolate or pull out some cold apple cider, and we all had a feast.

I remember one time in particular when the masses crowded into our house—it was near payday—she pulled me aside and asked, "Becky, what do we have to eat?" I said, "Orange soda pop, cheese, and crackers." She replied, "Then, that's what we'll have." And we did.

It's Not What's in the Plate

You see, what she was teaching all of us—from the new Christian to the old Christian—was that the family of God needs to be together, teaching, encouraging, and loving one another. It didn't matter what was on the table. The point was just to be around the table.

Years have passed, and hospitality is vanishing. Our agendas are too full, and with that our opportunities to grow spiritually have diminished. Too many times we have forgotten that Jesus, the Unseen Guest, joins His family, Christians, around the table, waiting to teach and love them, too: "Behold, I stand at the door and knock; if anyone hears My voice and opens the door, I will come in to him, and will dine with him, and he with Me" (Revelation 3:20).

Mom wrote these words about hospitality in her book, *Precious in the Sight of God:*

> Guests do not long remember the menu but rather the warmth or lack of warmth of the home. We can come closer to offending by too much "show" than by too sparse a meal . . . It is not what is in the plate that matters, but what's on the face of the hostess that counts! That takes a long time to learn . . . We need to be mindful that our houses will burn some day with all their furnishings and food, but the heart that continues to "burn with the desire to listen to Him" will someday sit at the table that He has gone to prepare for those who love Him (Fowler 98–99).

Oh, the many lessons Mom taught me. My precious sisters, we must leave a healthy, spiritual legacy for our daughters and sons. What examples are we setting for our own children as we and they rush in and back out the front door with such busy lifestyles? Do our children ever see us reading our Bibles, or is the big screen television blaring continuously? Do they see us gathered around the table and having wonderful, biblical discussions with our spiritual family, or is the kitchen closed? What memories will they take to their own homes?

What kind of table have we set before our children?

CHAPTER 3

Seek The Good Part

Seek the Lord while He may be found; call upon Him while he is near (Isaiah 55:6).

But seek first His kingdom and His righteousness; and all these things shall be added to you (Matthew 6:33).

Can you see her there, sitting at Jesus' feet, hanging on His every word? She is at home with her sister and brother, with the demands of visitors and the noise in the house. And there she sits. Her eyes are on Jesus. Nothing exists or matters but Him. Her sister keeps calling her. She is certainly neglecting her hostess duties, but she tunes her sister out. There are needs to be met, for the house is full of hungry guests, thirteen men at least, but she couldn't care less. All she sees is Him and His presence.

He is the most important man she has ever met. He is the Rabbi, the Master Teacher. And He is her friend. She understands something else that even His own apostles do not: He is the Son of God, and His time on earth is short.

Her name is Mary. She has a sister Martha and a brother Lazarus. Many scholars also assume that Simon, the leper of Mark 14, is their father, and that Jesus healed him. But that event is not recorded in the Bible. Mary's family lives in Bethany, a mere two miles from Jerusalem.

There is a special relationship between this family and the Messiah. The Gospel accounts of Jesus' life speak of His going to Bethany on more than one occasion, most likely escaping the demands of the crowds and the Pharisees, and finding refuge with Lazarus' family:

> Matthew 21:17—And He left them and went out of the city to Bethany, and spent the night there.
>
> Mark 11:11—Jesus entered Jerusalem and came into the temple; and after looking around at everything, He left for Bethany with the twelve, since it was already late.
>
> Mark 11:12—On the next day, when they had left Bethany, He became hungry.

NOWHERE TO LAY HIS HEAD

It is hard for us who live in the land of plenty to imagine the Palestinian world at the time Jesus lived. It seems that Jesus lived below the poverty level. One of the saddest scriptures to me is, "The foxes have holes and the birds of the air have nests, but the Son of Man has nowhere to lay His head" (Matthew 8:20).

How difficult to imagine not having a comfortable bed and two soft pillows for your head every night! But Jesus did not have that on earth. Not even a place to lay His head. I like to think that the home of Mary, Martha, and Lazarus provided the Savior of the world, the King of heaven, with some measure of comfort for His weary body—some quiet, some peace.

Notice the observations on Matthew 8:20 by two commentators: the first by Albert Barnes, and the second by Matthew Henry. Both of these references are online.

> The very foxes and birds, says he, have places of repose and shelter, but the Son of man has no home and no pillow. He is a stranger in his own world—a wanderer and an outcast from the homes of people.
>
> Our Lord Jesus submitted to the disgraces and distresses of extreme poverty. For our sakes he became poor, very poor. He had not a

> settlement, had not a place of repose, not a house of his own, to put his head in, not a pillow of his own, to lay his head on. He and his disciples lived on the charity of well-disposed people, that ministered to him of their substance . . . Christ submitted to this, not only that he might in all respects humble himself, and fulfill the scriptures, which spake of him as poor and needy, but that he might show us the vanity of worldly wealth, and teach us to look upon it with a holy contempt that he might purchase better things for us, and so make us rich.

THE ART OF LISTENING

I am thankful that God has given us this Bethany scene in the Bible. It is a short vignette—a tiny narrative of only five verses, but it packs a powerful punch for teaching all women. When I read it, I feel like the Lord is allowing us to eavesdrop on a personal, intimate scene unfolding in a home:

> Now as they were traveling along, He entered a village; and a woman named Martha welcomed Him into her home. She had a sister called Mary, who was seated at the Lord's feet, listening to His word. But Martha was distracted with all her preparations; and she came up to Him and said, "Lord, do You not care that my sister has left me to do all the serving alone? Then tell her to help me." But the Lord answered and said to her, "Martha, Martha, you are worried and bothered about so many things; but only one thing is necessary, for Mary has chosen the good part, which shall not be taken away from her" (Luke 10:38–42).

How many times have we read, heard, and studied this wonderful account? Many times, my friends. It is a favorite, particularly of women as it involves two sisters, Jesus, and a problem. Brother Marshall Keeble, an amazing preacher of yesteryear in the church, would often say to his audience about a passage, "Let's handle it and see what we can get out of it." Okay, brother Keeble, let's do just that.

1. *They were traveling along.* Who are *they*? They are Jesus and His apostles, going from town to town, teaching, healing, and helping

others. We are told that Jesus entered the village of Bethany where Mary and Martha lived, a little town not far from Jerusalem (John 11:1–18).

2. *Martha was distracted.* She invited and welcomed these men, at least thirteen of them, into her home and was soon all wrapped up in providing food for her guests. What she did was a good deed and no small task, to be sure! She looked around, and there was her sister Mary, sitting, of all things! Not helping her—but sitting! And where was Mary sitting? At Jesus' feet. Not at His side, wrapped up in a private conversation, but at His feet—the position of a humble student, a person who wants to learn.

3. *Mary was listening to Jesus' words.* Was she talking, laughing, and exchanging pleasantries while mingling with all the guests? No, Mary sat on the floor, probably looking up and hanging on to Jesus' every word. Can't you just imagine her, sitting there? Burton Coffman observed:

   > This has a dual meaning, namely, that Mary sat beneath Jesus on a lower seat; but it also has a figurative meaning of listening as a disciple would listen to a teacher (*Luke* 213).

DISTRACTED TO FRUSTRATION

Let's put on Martha's apron and imagine the scene in this Bethany home. Do you know what it is like to be busy in the kitchen and start frantically looking around for someone to help you? Sure you do. Every woman who reads this passage completely understands the scenario in Martha's kitchen that day! We have all been there, done that, and got the tee shirt!

It is not hard to imagine Martha's opening the cabinets, running around to get out the dishes and napkins, and then steam beginning to come out her ears as she turns and sees her little sister and what she is doing!

I chuckle when I imagine this scene, don't you? If this scene had happened at the Fowler home, with my older sister Judy in the kitchen and me in the living room totally involved in a teacher's words, everyone in our house would have heard what Judy had to say to me! Trust me. There would certainly have been a hot cook in our kitchen, and I would have been in hot water with her!

We all can feel Martha's frustration and her rising temper. The scriptures describe her as distracted by all her preparations. She was sidetracked with all the details. And that is easy for us to understand. Any woman who has ever helped with getting supper on the table for a crowd certainly knows these feelings of mounting hysteria. After all, didn't Martha welcome them? She was the hostess! I imagine the extreme tension Martha endured just to keep a smile on her face. Perhaps there was even a little gritting of the teeth!

Do you think Jesus knew what was going on in that kitchen in Bethany? Of course He did. He might have even been laughing to Himself as He watched the scene unwind, or do you think He watched the cook unwind? Whatever, Martha instantly drew Jesus in on her frustration.

Didn't Jesus have sisters who might have created a picture of frustration on numerous occasions? Isn't it possible that He had witnessed a similar scenario many times in Nazareth? I remember Mom saying that she thought that Jesus, as the oldest, had most likely been called in to stop some squabbles and arguments. Makes sense to me. Think outside the box, girls. Think what it was like for Jesus to grow up with at least four brothers and two sisters. "Is not this the carpenter, the son of Mary, and brother of James and Joses and Judas and Simon? Are not His sisters here with us?" (Mark 6:3).

Jesus knew about a family's inner workings because He had an earthly family. It is not hard to imagine that even Jesus had to make peace at times. Was this little tiff in Martha's house just like old times for our Messiah who grew up approximately seventy-seven miles away in Nazareth? Perhaps once again Jesus was intervening as an older brother working out a problem between two sisters. This was a natural role for

Him, don't you think? I cannot help but think that to the Lord, this Bethany family was just that—family.

DO YOU NOT CARE?

Look at what big sister Martha does now. She does not holler at Him from the kitchen but marches right up to Him and says, "Lord, do You not care that my sister has left me to do all the serving alone? Then tell her to help me."

How interesting that Martha first accuses Jesus of not caring about her predicament in the kitchen and then proceeds to order Jesus to talk to Mary and get things right! Do you know of any other time in the Bible that *a woman* orders the Lord to do something? The closest thing to this perhaps happened at the wedding in Cana when His mother Mary told Him to help with the wine problem. But here Martha tells Jesus exactly what to do: "Tell her to help me!"

Surely Jesus and Martha must have been good friends or she would not have acted this way. Martha felt comfortable enough with Jesus to tell Him what He needed to do! This is bold and it is humorous to us women as we study this event two thousand years later. Why? Because we identify with both Martha and Mary.

Before we get really upset with Martha, can we consider one thing? Where did Martha really want to be at this moment? Think. What did Martha really want to do? The very thing that her sister Mary was doing—sitting at the Master's feet, being in on the lively discussion, learning some more from the Master Teacher. But somebody had to get the food on the table.

ONLY ONE THING

Jesus softly chides Martha and reminds her that she is so concerned with many things but that only one thing is necessary. He says to her, "Mary has chosen the good part, which shall not be taken away from her" (Luke 10:42).

What is the one thing? What is the good part? It is Christ Jesus Himself. It is Immanuel, God with us, the Savior of all mankind. And there was nothing on the face of this earth that was going to come between Mary and her listening to her Savior. He had all the words of eternal life, and Mary was not going to miss a single one. Mary is the epitome of the eager student, the one whose heart's desire is to know more and more. Mary had chosen Him.

> The one thing needful. This can be nothing except hearing the word of the Lord; that is what Mary was doing, and it was the thing which Jesus refused to interrupt on behalf of lesser human obligation. The application is timeless: whatever the duties of men . . . the one great obligation of all who were ever born is that they shall heed the word of the Son of God. Much of the failure of modern Christianity lies in the fact that Christians are busy with all kinds of things, but yet they have no time for the word of the Lord (Coffman, *Luke* 214).

Jesus' lesson of priorities in that cozy home hits all of us, doesn't it? Too many times we get caught up in the preparation of physical food and don't see the real food right before our eyes. We don't see that it is time to drop everything, sit down, and feed our spiritual souls.

> It is not true that Martha was an unspiritual person, for one of the noblest confessions of faith in the New Testament was made by her (John 11:27); but in the incident here, she was indignant at what appeared in her eyes as a slight of duty on Mary's part, and she called for the Lord to rebuke it. Nor do the Lord's words deny that a duty had been neglected; but, rather, they stress that a higher duty had been honored by Mary. It is the setting aside of lesser duties for the observance of higher duties that appears to be Luke's reason for including this intimate, revealing story of two sisters (Coffman, *Luke* 213).

For example, it is easy for women to get carried away in the decorating, the food, and the favors at a ladies' day. "Make it simple" is my motto. How easy it is to be a Martha and get distracted by all the committees and the details of the day and miss out on meeting the Lord in the auditorium! Have sandwiches or crockpots full of soup and an easy cleanup so that learning can continue in the assembly. I love it when the gentlemen help in the kitchen so that the ladies can be free to enjoy their times together and sit at the Lord's feet. Thank you, my brothers!

LASTING MEMORY OF THE LAST TIME

Here is one more scene in the friendship of Mary, Martha, Lazarus, and Jesus. Observe once more the love Jesus had for that special little family and the love they most assuredly had for Him. As His life drew to a close and Calvary was just hours away, Jesus found Himself at their home for the last time.

> Jesus, therefore, six days before the Passover, came to Bethany where Lazarus was, whom Jesus had raised from the dead. So they made Him a supper there, and Martha was serving; but Lazarus was one of those reclining at the table with Him. Mary then took a pound of very costly perfume of pure nard, and anointed the feet of Jesus and wiped His feet with her hair; and the house was filled with the fragrance of the perfume. But Judas Iscariot, one of His disciples, who was intending to betray Him, said, "Why was this perfume not sold for three hundred denarii and given to poor people?" Now he said this, not because he was concerned about the poor, but because he was a thief, and as he had the money box, he used to pilfer what was put into it. Therefore Jesus said, "Let her alone, so that she may keep it for the day of My burial. For you always have the poor with you, but you do not always have Me" (John 12:1–8).

Mark's account adds these words about Mary:

> She has done what she could; she has anointed My body beforehand for the burial. Truly I say to you, wherever the gospel is preached in the whole world, what this woman has done will also be spoken of in memory of her (Mark 14:8–9).

Do you see a difference in the John 12 account and the previous account in Luke 10? There are many similarities: many people, food to be prepared, two sisters and a brother, and the Master. But there is peace now. Lessons have been learned.

Mary anointed Jesus with spikenard, an extremely expensive ointment from India. It's interesting to note that only John's account records that the house was filled with the fragrance of the perfume (John 12:3). Read this and pause as you picture the moment; you can almost smell the fragrance.

And only Mark's account records Jesus' beautiful statement about Mary. Notice the main phrases:

- She has done what she could
- Wherever the gospel is preached
- Spoken of in memory of her

How true! Her deed became a memorial. Don't we still remember and discuss Mary's touching demonstration of her love for our Lord?

SEEK THE GOOD PART

Can't you see Jesus' deep love for this family? They offered Him respite—an escape from the hatred spewing from the self-righteous Pharisees, the hypocritical Sadducees, and Satan himself. Here was a family who loved Him with all their hearts and even called Him in to share their grief. A family that made Jesus one of the family!

Together Mary and Martha were quite a team. They both wanted to give, and they both wanted to serve the most precious Friend in the world. These sisters were true givers and servants—Pearl Seekers.

Let's always remember this: Both Mary and Martha were Pearl Seekers of the highest calling. They would do anything possible to listen to the Messiah. Will we do the same thing? Do we hang on to His words and seek Him through the Word of God? Is Jesus the good part in our lives?

What was it like to have the Son of God knock on your door on a regular basis? I can't even imagine. I have to ask myself, "Would the Lord be comfortable in my home and sitting at my table?"

> We need to be mindful that our houses will burn someday with all their furnishings and food, but the heart that continues to burn with desire to listen to Him will someday sit at the table He has gone to prepare for those who love Him (Fowler 99).

When I get to heaven, I would love to sit at Martha and Mary's table and visit with them. How wonderful it would be to just do lunch for a couple of thousand years with my sisters from long ago!

Mary and Martha, how thankful we sisters are that God has given us your life examples in the Bible! We never tire of studying you. We not only identify with you, but we feel like we understand you. Through both of you, women see Pearl Seekers of the first century, and we marvel at your examples of hospitality, priorities, and true love. How blessed you were to get to know Christ Himself! We feel that we are kindred spirits, and we long to meet you. When you set the table tonight in heaven, please set a place for us. We will be there soon.

Prayer: Lord, help me to seek the good part!

Song: Because He Lives

God sent His Son, they called Him Jesus;
He came to love, heal and forgive;
He lived and died to buy my pardon,
An empty grave is there to prove my Savior lives!

Chorus:
Because He lives, I can face tomorrow,
Because He lives, all fear is gone;
Because I know He holds the future,
And life is worth the living,
Just because He lives!

How sweet to hold a newborn baby,
And feel the pride and joy he gives;
But greater still the calm assurance:
This child can face uncertain days because He lives!

And then one day, I'll cross the river,
I'll fight life's final war with pain;
And then, as death gives way to victory,
I'll see the lights of glory and I'll know He lives!

Digging for Pearls

1. Why do you think Jesus frequently visited the Bethany home of Mary and Martha?

2. Discuss the possibilities of Jesus' thoughts as He watched the conflict unfold between Mary and Martha?

3. How easy is it to get distracted like Martha and get caught up in details? How do you handle similar pressure?

Pearl Drop

Step Over the Line, Sister!

Most Americans know something about the Alamo, but Texans can tell you everything about it. A small, distinctive adobe mission, the Alamo represents heroism and freedom at its best. It's a story of bravery against impossible odds, and it's a place of sacred ground in America's history.

You know the story, don't you? Brave men, Davy Crockett, Col. William B. Travis, and Jim Bowie, along with some two hundred weathered, seasoned soldiers, who had fought many a battle, determined that Texas should have its freedom from Mexico. That small group of rebels gathered for their last stand in the Alamo's complex—a church and small buildings joined by a common outer wall. General Santa Anna and his troops, numbering anywhere from a thousand to six thousand men, surrounded them, and both sides dug in for the siege that lasted thirteen days. When hope for reinforcements ran out, the small band of men knew their end was near.

On March 5, 1836, Colonel Travis, only twenty-six years of age, bravely gathered his men. Drawing a line in the sand with his sword, he challenged those who would fight and die with him to step over that line. Every man except one—he went home—stepped over Travis' line. Even the sick and ailing Jim Bowie had his men lift his bed and place it over the line. This must have been a very moving and dramatic moment. Some historians doubt the story's authenticity, but we do know that Travis gave his men the opportunity to stay or leave.

In the early morning hours of March 6, 1836, the Mexican army stormed the compound and killed every man in the small group. The cry, "Remember the Alamo," became the battle cry of the Texians who finally won Texas' independence at the battle of San Jacinto on April 21, 1836.

I tell you this story because there is a definite parallel here for the Christian life. God has drawn a line in the sand for us humans. We have the choice either to be His or to belong to Satan. It's that simple.

When we obey the gospel of Jesus and become Christians, we spiritually step over the line. We make the deliberate choice to be buried with Christ in baptism and begin the Christian life. One does not become a Christian by accident. It is a deliberate act. It is "on purpose."

We kill the old girl and we become that new girl God has in mind for us. There is a death involved here! Like Christ died, we die, and we are raised with Him to begin our new life—from here to eternity.

> Therefore we have been buried with Him through baptism into death, so that as Christ was raised from the dead through the glory of the Father, so we too might walk in newness of life (Romans 6:4).

> Now if we have died with Christ, we believe that we shall also live with Him, knowing that Christ, having been raised from the dead, is never to die again; death no longer is master over Him. For the death that He died, He died to sin once for all; but the life that He lives, He lives to God. Even so consider yourselves to be dead to sin, but alive to God in Christ Jesus (Romans 6:8–11).

We cannot look back. We are committed to God as a soldier and a family member. We have our eyes fixed on Him:

> Therefore, since we have so great a cloud of witnesses surrounding us, let us also lay aside every encumbrance and the sin which so easily entangles us, and let us run with endurance the race that is set before us, fixing our eyes on Jesus, the author and perfecter of faith, who for the joy set before Him endured the cross, despising the shame, and has sat down at the right hand of the throne of God (Hebrews 12:1–2).

What is ahead of us is so much better than our present condition. The Christian's future is tremendous and unimaginable—full of hope and glory.

Inspired by the Holy Spirit, both the prophet Isaiah and the apostle Paul wrote these amazing words: "Things which eye has not seen and ear has not heard, and which have not entered the heart of man, all that God has prepared for those who love Him" (Isaiah 64:4; 1 Corinthians 2:9).

On the other hand, the unbeliever's future is unthinkable. One can argue all day long, saying, "There is no God; there is no Jesus; there is no gospel; and even, there is no hell." But I challenge all of us to look at these most chilling verses. (Italics is mine.)

> For after all it is only just for God to repay with affliction those who afflict you, and to give relief to you who are afflicted and to us as well when the Lord Jesus will be revealed from heaven with His mighty angels in flaming fire, *dealing out retribution to those who do not know God and to those who do not obey the gospel of our Lord Jesus. These will pay the penalty of eternal destruction,* away from the presence of the Lord and from the glory of His power (2 Thessalonians 1:6–9).

Don't dwell on the sorrows and troubles of the day, my sweet sister. We shall always have them (Matthew 6:34). Think, and think again about what lies ahead for us.

Brother Marshall Keeble was known to say, "God voted for you. Satan voted against you. Now you get to cast the deciding vote." What will you do with Jesus, my friend? Make the most important decision you will ever make. Step over the line, Christian. It's time to stand for the Truth, and it's time to be His.

CHAPTER 4

Seek
A Spiritual Mindset

Ezra opened the book in the sight of all the people for he was standing above all the people; and when he opened it, all the people stood up. Then Ezra blessed the Lord the great God. And all the people answered, "Amen, Amen!" while lifting up their hands; then they bowed low and worshiped the Lord with their faces to the ground (Nehemiah 8:5–6).

I figure that the Bible works like this: If you get a book named after you, you surely must be special! And you certainly did something God liked! I just don't see any rough, immoral, and rebellious characters with their name on a book in the Old Testament or the New Testament, do you?

God inspired good men—holy men—to write down His words and thoughts and admonitions.

> Knowing this first, that no prophecy of Scripture is of any private interpretation, for prophecy never came by the will of man, but holy men of God spoke as they were moved by the Holy Spirit (2 Peter 1:20–21 NKJV).

Matthew, Mark, Luke, and John were excellent authors, recording events in the life of Christ. Job, Isaiah, Jeremiah, and Daniel were righteous men who not only obeyed God but also were examples of strength and great faith. Esther and Ruth were women of integrity who put God first in their lives. Each has his or her name on a book in the Bible. But let us always remember that these outstanding characters were also human and imperfect. We must never forget the fact that God uses ordinary men and women—like you and me—to accomplish His will.

EZRA'S CREDENTIALS

One of my Bible heroes is Ezra. He is honored with his own book. Ezra was an outstanding scribe who loved God and wanted to please Him. He was gifted with an excellent pedigree—he could trace his ancestors all the way back to Aaron, the first high priest—sixteen generations of the Levitical priesthood.

Let's look into Ezra's biography:

> Now after these things, in the reign of Artaxerxes king of Persia, there went up Ezra son of Seraiah, son of Azariah, son of Hilkiah, son of Shallum, son of Zadok, son of Ahitub, son of Amariah, son of Azariah, son of Meraioth, son of Zerahiah, son of Uzzi, son of Bukki, son of Abishua, son of Phinehas, son of Eleazar, son of Aaron the chief priest.
>
> This Ezra went up from Babylon, and he was a scribe skilled in the law of Moses, which the Lord God of Israel had given; and the king granted him all he requested because the hand of the Lord his God was upon him. Some of the sons of Israel and some of the priests, the Levites, the singers, the gatekeepers and the temple servants went up to Jerusalem in the seventh year of King Artaxerxes (Ezra 7:1–7).

Underline the definition of a scribe. List four characteristics of scribes skilled in the law of Moses.

____

____

____

____

____

____

____

Note the following observation from Merrill Tenny:

> Scribes [were] persons employed to handle correspondence and to keep accounts. They were given a high place alongside the high priest. Hezekiah set up a body of men

> whose work it was to transcribe old records, or to put in writing what had been handed down orally (Proverbs 25:1). The scribe came to be a student and interpreter of the law. In the time of Christ, the scribes had attained great influence and power as a class, and were regarded with great respect. They were given the best places at feasts and the chief seats in the synagogues (Matthew 23:6; Luke 14:7) (599).

Scribes were men from the tribe of Levi who were versed in the Mosaic law, even being called lawyers by many. They made official documents by copying the laws of the land and the laws of God. Ezra 7:6 tells us that Ezra was a ready scribe (KJV). What does that mean? The Hebrew word that is translated "ready" means skilled, quick, prompt, and ready. Ezra was a scribe who was skilled in the law of God. He was an excellent student and a fine scholar! Today we would say, "He really knew his stuff!" or "He had a PhD in Bible!" Keeble would say, "He'd had his brain expanded!"

WHAT WAS IN HIS HAND?

What books of law were in Ezra's Old Testament? We know he was well acquainted with the Torah, the first five books that God inspired Moses to write.

In Ezra 7 we see him traveling with a great number of exiled Jews returning to Jerusalem, thanks to the goodness of King Artaxerxes. That must have been quite a scene.

Let us look at a portion of the letter from the king:

> Forasmuch as you are sent by the king and his seven counselors to inquire concerning Judah and Jerusalem according to the law of your God which is in your hand (Ezra 7:14).

Ezra had a copy of God's law in his own hand. What a bundle of information God has given us in this verse, revealing to us that the law of God was still alive, and had survived the seventy-year Babylonian captivity! Here is what Burton Coffman has to say about God's Word and its survival:

> It is significant that he had a copy of the Law of Moses; and this, we may believe, was also true of many faithful descendants of Aaron through the long centuries between the Exodus and the return from Babylon . . . That Ezra was in full possession of the Torah indicates the preservation of it through the ages (*Ezra* 59–60).

Ezra had taken great care of the law he inherited. Let us make sure that we understand that Ezra's copy of the law was not a leather-bound book the size of our Bibles today. The law of the Lord was preserved on parchment or papyrus scrolls which were rolled up for storage or transporting. These scrolls were big, heavy, and bulky. Can you imagine the intense caution with which Ezra not only handled the scrolls but also copied them for the people of God?

SPIRITUAL MINDSET

Now let us look closely into Ezra's character:

> He came to Jerusalem in the fifth month, which was in the seventh year of the king. For on the first of the first month he began to go up from Babylon; and on the first of the fifth month he came to Jerusalem, because the good hand of his God was upon him. For Ezra had set his heart to study the law of the Lord and to practice it, and to teach His statutes and ordinances in Israel (Ezra 7:8–10).

The distance from Babylon to Jerusalem was 520 miles, as the crow flies. But that route was impractical, most of it being across an unsympathetic desert. The practical route passed northwest through the Tigris-Euphrates valley to Haran, and then south to Jerusalem—900 miles. The trip took four months.

Many Jews accompanied Ezra. They passed through several countries, so those governments were appeased, and many enemies were confronted. But God blessed Ezra all along, for both verses 6 and 9 tell us that the hand of the Lord his God was upon him. God certainly had a plan for Ezra and blessed his every move back to Jerusalem. Why?

> For Ezra had set his heart to study the law of the Lord and to practice it, and to teach His statutes and ordinances in Israel (Ezra 7:10).

In this text, the word *for* is a coordinating conjunction; it means because. We can absolutely restate verses 9 and 10 to say, "The good hand of his God was upon him, because Ezra had set his heart to study the law of the Lord and to practice it, and to teach His statutes and ordinances in Israel."

This is a zinger passage that I love. It leaps right off the page. Why was Ezra so blessed to be traveling back home to Israel with power and riches given to him by the most powerful king in the world? Why? Because God had His hand upon him. Why? Because Ezra had set his heart on God. Ezra had made up his mind to know everything he could know about God's Word.

> The events centered around the name of Ezra must be accounted among the most wonderful things that ever happened to God's people. The immense dimensions of Ezra's request of Artaxerxes stagger the imagination; and the authority given to Ezra by that monarch, making him, in fact, ruler of the entire province beyond the River, with the power of life and death to enforce his reforms appears to have been directly the result of Divine favor and intervention, as positively indicated by Ezra's thanksgiving at the end of the chapter (Coffman, *Ezra* 59).

I have read verse 10 many times, and all I can say is, "Wow! What a man!" But wait. Let's look at this verse again. Ezra had purposed three things in his heart:

1. to study God's law

2. to practice it—to live it

3. to teach it wherever he went in Israel

Make sure you notice the correct order here: first, study the law; then, live the law; then, teach the law. Ezra was going to practice what he preached, and that sermon was straight from the Book! Period.

KNOW IT, LIVE IT, TEACH IT

Why wouldn't God love a man such as Ezra? He had set the course of his life to know the law of God, to live it, and then to teach it. Be sure to notice that Ezra was determined to teach God's law, not Ezra's law. He didn't have a hidden agenda for promoting himself, his beliefs, and his interpretations. Many men study the law of God but then refuse to teach it; or they teach it and refuse to live it. Knowing isn't doing! Ezra was an outstanding man: a pupil, a doer, and then a teacher.

How I wish we all had the same insatiable desire for the knowledge of the Bible that Ezra had! How remarkable it would be for all people to determine to know God's commandments, live God's commandments, and then teach God's commandments! I truly believe that if Ezra's three goals were embraced by Christians today, the entire world would be evangelized over and over! Just think of the vast number of Christians that could exist, if each Christian craved to be a real Pearl Seeker, a seeker of everything God has to offer!

You and I can only speculate how and when Ezra arrived at this spiritual mindset. It seems that this had been on Ezra's heart for many years. Surely he prayed to God for help. It wasn't some impetuous and haphazard idea.

I try to imagine Ezra in a foreign country, taking time to pull out the scrolls of law and read them again and again. No doubt, he knew Genesis, Exodus, Leviticus, Numbers, Deuteronomy, Joshua, and Judges backward, forward, and upside down. Remember, he was a skilled scribe. He had cut his teeth on the Torah before he ever got to Jerusalem! But that was not enough for Ezra. His heart's desire was to know more about God and do more for Him.

SEEK THE WORD: HEARING AND DOING

God inspired James to write in James 1:22: "But prove yourselves doers of the word, and not merely hearers who delude themselves." Although Ezra lived hundreds of years before James wrote his book, he was living proof of this scripture. The example of Ezra shouts volumes to us over the centuries. He is the epitome of God's Bible student and God's Bible teacher. Ezra was a Pearl Seeker.

Oh, how we Christians need to hunger for the Word and have the same desire to increase our knowledge of the Bible. We will never understand or comprehend it all, that is for sure. However, can't we too set our minds on learning more? Sure we can, but will we?

I do know this: If we are hungry for more spiritual knowledge, God will see that we find it. Jesus said in Matthew 5:6, "Blessed are those who hunger and thirst for righteousness, for they shall be satisfied." My personal translation of this scripture is, "Happy are those who are hungry and thirsty for righteousness, for they will get their answers!"

> There is no thirst like that of the soul for the knowledge of God. Only the knowledge and assurance of God and the maintenance of our human relationship with Him can save an intelligent soul from insanity. God is our Life; he is the Light of the world; he is the fountain of living waters; He is our All in All; as Augustine said it, "Our souls, O God, were made for Thee; and never shall they rest until they rest in Thee" (Coffman, *Psalms*).

Can you imagine how much Ezra yearned to go back to Jerusalem, the city of David? Here he could help his people Israel to begin again: renewing proper worship, rededicating God's law, and rebuilding the people of God. Surely he considered it beyond his wildest dreams to be able to worship God freely and to study to his heart's content. But God being God, He knew the heart of Ezra and said yes to him. He gave Ezra the complete freedom to accomplish such a dream.

Prayer: Lord, help me to have a spiritual mindset.

Song: Give Me the Bible

Give me the Bible, star of gladness gleaming,
To cheer the wand'rer lone and tempest tossed;
No storm can hide that radiance peaceful beaming,
Since Jesus came to seek and save the lost.

Chorus:
Give me the Bible, holy message shining;
Thy light shall guide me in the narrow way;
Precept and promise, law and love combining,
Till night shall vanish in eternal day.

Give me the Bible, when my heart is broken,
When sin and grief have filled my soul with fear;
Give me the precious words by Jesus spoken,
Hold up faith's lamp to show my Savior near.

Give me the Bible, all my steps enlighten,
Teach me the danger of these realms below;
That lamp of safety o'er the gloom shall brighten,
That light alone the path of peace can show.

Give me the Bible, lamp of life immortal,
Hold up that splendor by the open grave;
Show me the light from Heaven's shining portal,
Show me the glory gilding Jordan's wave.

Digging for Pearls

1. Describe a scribe.

2. Why would God love a man such as Ezra?

3. Name some ways God blessed Ezra.

Pearl Drop

What Is More Important Than God?

It is impossible to describe the beauty of New England. You have most likely seen the postcards and the calendars with the breathtaking scenes of the roaring ocean, the majestic snow-capped mountains, the vibrant colors of autumn, the tree-rimmed lakes, and the snow scenes straight from a Currier and Ives painting. You may try to depict life in that part of Americana, its people, its mentality, and its dynamics to other Americans, but you will never be able to do so adequately. Your friends will never be able to see the word picture you are trying to paint for them. That is because only New Englanders know New England. You must live there to grasp it. You must experience it.

The Lord blessed us in Concord, New Hampshire. He provided for us and enabled us to establish a congregation for Him. For several years the church met in our basement. Then Dad designed and erected a church building next door. Our lives were full of company, gospel meetings, and nonstop Bible classes.

In the summertime we had an amazing vacation Bible school! Since Mom was a well-known music teacher in two nearby communities, she and Dad could easily knock on doors and invite families to send their kids to our VBS. Dad would somehow rent a school bus and pick up all the children. Our average attendance was well over a hundred every day.

We were known as the "Popsicle School," and every kid around wanted to attend! During the morning break, everyone got a frozen popsicle—which was a definite draw for most children. It was the ideal snack for a summer church school. We let the kids out for a break, fed them a popsicle, and then

hosed them off before returning for a second lesson inside. It worked great for us!

Since the VBS was quite large, we always needed teachers. Many times sponsoring congregations from the South sent their elders and wives, preachers, and other volunteers. We always had a houseful of guests, and we tried to show them the sights of New England.

Golf, Golf, and No More Golf

One summer a Texas congregation sent its preacher, two elders, and their wives to help us. They were an unusual group, vibrant personalities and lots of fun. We thoroughly enjoyed them.

We taught VBS classes every morning. Then in the afternoon we went out to see (and taste) as many tourist attractions as possible. However, Mike—the Texas preacher—was a golfer. Everything he talked about concerned golf. He told us a lot of funny jokes—all about golf. He had a wonderful sense of humor, and his stories made us laugh.

At the end of the first day's classes, my parents extended an invitation to Mike: "Hey, want to go and see the rockbound coast of Maine this afternoon?"

"No, I have to go play golf!" he replied. So we left him and went down the road to get to the cold Atlantic Ocean to savor a lobster and some homemade ice cream.

Next day my parents offered another invitation: "Hey, Mike, want to go to the White Mountains of New Hampshire with us and see the Old Man of the Mountains that Nathaniel Hawthorne wrote about? Want to see his face carved on the side of the mountain?" (By the way, his face has since fallen off.)

"No, I can't. I have to go and play golf!" So off we went without Mike.

Invitations and rejections continued daily. At the end of the week, Mike, the elders, and their wives said their goodbyes and headed back to Texas. We were very sad to see them go, for we had loved having them in our home. They had become part of our family.

Several years later, my parents were attending a Christian college lectureship when they ran into Mike! It was a joyous reunion. Then Mom asked, "Mike, how is your golf game these days?"

Mike replied, "Lea, I don't play golf anymore."

Mom was shocked! She said, "You don't play golf anymore? What happened?"

Mike said, "It became more important than God." You see, Mike had hit a roadblock in his walk with God. Everything in his world was revolving around golf. Every waking minute was consumed with hitting the greens. Mike came to realize that golf had become bigger and more important than God, his family, his commitment to the brethren—everything. He was missing out on life—his life. When it came to "walking the walk," Mike was playing the wrong game, for every road he took led to the clubhouse.

Every Sunday Mike had been teaching others to follow the Lord while he himself was traveling in the opposite direction. Every Sunday Mike was preaching to his congregation about keeping spiritual priorities straight while his priorities were haywire. God had taken a back seat in Mike's golf cart, and little did Mike realize that his life was seriously stuck in Satan's sand trap. Fortunately, Mike was mature enough to see the signs of impending doom and climbed out of the pit in time.

God in the Back Seat

My sisters, there is a parallel here for you and me. As Christians, we too can do the very same thing with the Lord, our priorities, and the promises we make to Him by becoming enamored with the world. We invite God the Father, God the Son, and God the Holy Spirit into our lives. They come into our living room and we say to them, "Oh, sit here on my couch. We are going to have such a wonderful time together! We are going to talk and pray and read the Bible. We are going to spend hours and hours together. This is going to be great!

"Oh, wait just a minute. I have to run to the store and get some cream of mushroom soup for tonight's casserole, but I will be right back.

And oh, I have to go and get the kids from school, but I will be right back. You just sit right there and I will be back in a minute!"

And God, Jesus, and the Holy Spirit wait, and they wait, and they wait. And one of these days, my sisters, the time will be up! There will be no more time to talk and pray and read the Bible with the Godhead because eternity will have arrived, and we will stand before the Father, Son, and the Holy Spirit with our foolish, pathetic, and idiotic excuses.

What did God say to the rich fool in Luke 12 who thought he had all the time in the world? "'You fool! This very night your soul is required of you; and now who will own what you have prepared?' So is the man who stores up treasure for himself, and is not rich toward God" (Luke 12:20–21).

Jehovah God called the rich man a fool. Why? Because the rich man's priorities were all out of whack. He thought only of himself, never of helping anyone else. He selfishly wanted more and more and more, never realizing that amassing things and looking out for "number one" violate everything Jesus stands for. The rich man thought he would be able to take his ease and eat, drink, and be merry. Instead, he died that very night.

Someone once said, "Worldliness is misplaced priorities." When worldly things become more important than God, we are in big trouble! I may not play golf, but I sure can let other things become my "god." How easy it is to get all wrapped up in various kinds of shopping, my children's and grandchildren's lives, sports, trips, and—you name it! And God takes a back seat in my Camry.

Fantastic Fans

My husband and I were once on an airplane packed with college football fans. They were the most obnoxious, irritating people I have ever seen. They shouted back and forth across the aisles, gloating over past bowl games, trips, and touchdowns. This was an 8:30 AM flight and most of these fans had already been drinking heavily. Just to think of the money they had spent for the weekend alone was staggering: plane tickets, game tickets, car rentals, motel rooms, food, and who knows what else! And they were set to do it all over again the next weekend. All I could think was, "Oh, how I wish people loved the Lord the way they love football!"

Each of those fans had probably spent at least a thousand dollars for one weekend of pleasure, and they were certainly willing to spend more. They knew every player, the stats, and the team's history. No price was too much for them in order to experience the game of football—live and in living color.

Imagine just for a moment what life would be like if we loved the Lord in that same manner. What if we spent our money traveling to lectureships, meetings, seminars, and gatherings that were designed to mature us? What if we were skilled in knowing what the Bible says—the stats of the Old and New Testament? What if planes took us to mission fields, and what if we, as salt and light for Christ, talked about our Savior to others across the aisles? Just imagine all the good we could do and the souls that would be saved!

When we focus on ourselves and our desires instead of our relationship with God, we miss the mark completely. We create our own personal *Titanic*. We board the ship and gleefully sink to the bottom of a freezing, cold ocean while the orchestra plays "Nearer My God to Thee."

How tragic to imagine God's looking at any of us and saying, "What were you thinking? What was more important than spending time with Me? I had so much I wanted to tell you! You wouldn't believe the life I had in mind for you, but you loved the world more than Me."

Oh, my sisters, if our souls were required of us this very night, would our Father call us fools?

Notable Quotes

If I shut up the heavens so that there is no rain, or if I command the locust to devour the land, or if I send pestilence among My people, and My people who are called by My name humble themselves and pray and seek My face and turn from their wicked ways, then I will hear from heaven, will forgive their sin and will heal their land.

—2 Chronicles 7:13–14

Do you know how many homes in the U.S. have a Bible? Nine out of ten. However, despite having a Bible in the home, only 37% report reading it once a week or more. Of those who read their Bible, only 57% say that it made them think about how to apply it each day. Many people are simply not opening their Bibles and allowing God to speak to them.

—Wellspring blog by
Teresa Hampton

One of the most powerful verses in the whole Bible is also one of the saddest. Listen as the Father lovingly pleads with His rebellious children to come home and then hear their foolish response:

> Thus says the Lord, "Stand by the ways and see and ask for the ancient paths, where the good way is, and walk in it; and you will find rest for your souls. But they said, 'We will not walk in it'" (Jeremiah 6:16).

Somehow I can hear the sorrow in God's voice as He speaks to His insubordinate children in Hosea 4:6: "My people are destroyed for lack of knowledge."

—Becky Blackmon

The righteous . . . will flourish like the palm tree . . . They will still yield fruit in old age.

—Psalm 92:12, 14

I want God to use me as long as I live, and I want to live so that God can use me.

—Marshall Keeble, at age 87

CHAPTER 5

Seek Second Chances

For though by this time you ought to be teachers, you have need again for someone to teach you the elementary principles of the oracles of God, and you have come to need milk and not solid food. For everyone who partakes only of milk is not accustomed to the word of righteousness, for he is an infant. But solid food is for the mature, who because of practice have their senses trained to discern good and evil (Hebrews 5:12–14).

YOU SHOULD BE ASHAMED!

Let's jump into the deep end and reflect for a moment on the state of the nation of Israel in Ezra's day. The northern kingdom abandoned God first, so God gave their king Hoshea into the hands of Shalmaneser, king of Assyria, "and Hoshea became his servant, and paid him tribute" (2 Kings 17:3).

Then Judah, the southern kingdom, played the harlot in every imaginable way. They no longer worshiped or sacrificed in a pleasing manner. The priests were immoral and very corrupt, and Solomon's temple became a place of prostitution and sacrifices to other gods.

God's children sacrificed their own children to Molech, the god of the Ammonites (2 Kings 17:17). What abominations occurred! After sending prophet after prophet to remind His people not only of His forgiving love but also of the consequences to come, the children of God wanted nothing to do with God. They were not ashamed of their wickedness, could not even blush, and boldly told God, "We will not obey." How utterly brazen for God's own children to turn their backs on Him!

> "Were they ashamed because of the abomination they have done? They were not even ashamed at all; they did not even know how to blush. Therefore they shall fall among those who fall; at the time that I punish them, they shall be cast down," says the Lord.
>
> Thus says the Lord, "Stand by the ways and see and ask for the ancient paths, where the good way is, and walk in it; and you will find rest for your souls. But they said, 'We will not walk in it.' And I set watchmen over you, saying, 'Listen to the sound of the trumpet!' But they said, 'We will not listen'" (Jeremiah 6:15–17).

God finally had enough. He allowed King Nebuchadnezzar of Babylon to conquer Jerusalem and carry His children away into captivity. Everything the prophets foretold occurred. (Don't you wonder how many Jews heard the prophets' voices ringing in their heads as they painfully made their way from their beloved land to captivity in Babylon?)

SECOND CHANCE—SEVENTY YEARS LATER

Our God is a God of second chances, isn't He? Surely we see this over and over in the Bible. Seventy years after God separated His people from their beloved Jerusalem, He had mercy on Israel and orchestrated their return to Jerusalem through the kindness of King Cyrus. Later Ezra returned with the blessing of King Artaxerxes. Slowly but surely groups of Jews returned home.

Once again, God opened His arms and welcomed His chastised children into His embrace. Israel needed a godly leader:

- A man who descended from Aaron the high priest.
- A man who knew the law, loved the law, and lived the law.
- A man who had the strength to rebuild and rule God's people.

- A man who would show Judah she needed to repent and get right with God.

- A man who would be a holy priest that was not perverted and immoral.

That man was Ezra. Read again his credentials and mission in Ezra 7. Who among them wanted to please God more than he? Ezra was the right man for the job that had to be accomplished immediately. Here was a rare man who had made up his mind to study, practice, and teach the Word of God, the Truth. Oh, for such men in our world today!

You see, girls, this pact that Ezra made with himself so long ago is called living for God. It is called total commitment. Ezra certainly was not the first man to make such a decision, and he certainly will not be the last.

On the first day of the first month he began to go up from Babylon, and on the first of the fifth month he came to Jerusalem, because the good hand of his God was upon him. For Ezra had set his heart to study the Law of the Lord, and to practice it, and to teach His statutes and ordinances in Israel.

—Ezra 7:9–10

STEP BY STEP

How do we live for God today? Becoming a Christian is the first step; making up one's mind to study God's Word is the next step; living an obedient life is the following step, along with telling others about the Lord. All of these steps will guide the child of God safely home to the Father's arms. How true it is: "The Lord is good to those who wait for Him, to the person who seeks Him" (Lamentations 3:25). Yes, God blesses the Pearl Seeker in many ways.

What a wonderful example Ezra has set before us of being such a fantastic student of the Word! He made up his mind to study, and then he did it. Can't we do the very same thing? Of course we can. But how many will choose to study the Bible? How many will even choose to read the Bible? More than that, how many will obey the words breathed from the lips of God?

As a young girl, I saw my parents sitting in the living room, reading their Bibles aloud together. It was a daily occurrence. They read and then discussed what they had read. Reading the Bible was part of their daily walk with God, and they never would have dreamed of neglecting it. I saw their faith in God increase day by day, and I observed the relationship they had with the Lord as it steadily grew.

My parents stressed the importance of God's Word to us children and taught us to be daily Bible readers from an early age. Dad even constructed a Bible Barometer for the foyer of the church building, so that every member and visitor could record his daily Bible reading habits and log in the chapters that he read. Dad's visual reminder encouraged kids and adults alike to strive for a hundred percent participation in the reading of the Word.

STAND OR FALL

Are you a daily Bible reader, my friend? Do you stop every day and read something from the Word of God? I always say, "If we took a poll of how many Christians are daily Bible readers, we would be shocked!" The number is very low. Isn't that sad? I sometimes wonder how we would act if we were persecuted and had our Bibles taken away. Would we panic? Would we beg others to come and supply us with more? Would we be able to recite any verses by memory?

God's precious Word tells us in Romans 10:17, "So faith comes from hearing, and hearing by the word of Christ." How remarkable it is to realize that our faith is growing and maturing as we stay in the Bible and become good students of the Book! Let's turn that around for a moment. What happens to our faith if we are not in the Bible? It becomes weak, and so do we.

Paul was inspired to write to the church at Colossae: "Let the word of Christ richly dwell within you" (Colossians 3:16). Tell me then, is it possible to let the word of Christ dwell within you poorly? Of course it is. What can happen as a result of our weakness in the Word? As teenagers we used to say, "We will fall for anything that comes down the pike!" It all sounds good. What is that old saying, "People who don't stand for anything will fall for everything"? I heard a strong man of faith once say, "When growth stops, decay begins!"

YOUR CHANCE FOR TIME-SHARE

What is so important in our daily lives that we do not have time to stop and read something from God's marvelous book? If we gave God the same amount of time we dedicate to Facebook, emails, television, and texts, we would have more than enough time for daily Bible reading! We must examine our priorities every day and set God on the throne of our hearts and minds. God will never accept second place!

Simply choosing other activities over the opportunities we have every single day to draw closer to God through prayer and Bible study reveals how we really feel about our Father. We would never dream of saying, "I don't love you, God." That is abhorrent to us. But living day after day without connecting with Him shouts volumes about what we really do love. Thomas Aquinas, a thirteenth century Italian theologian, observed: "The things we love tell us what we are!"

> No person can reach his spiritual potential without continually accessing God's power. Jesus' quiet moments of communion with the Father help to account for His undaunted courage. People who confine their petition and praise to one or two days a week are not serious about modeling their lives after Jesus (Johnson 154).

SHINE AS LIGHTS

Mom was the best Bible student and teacher I have ever known! Like Ezra, she dedicated herself to studying the Bible, living the Bible, and teaching the Bible. She told me again and again: "Becky, whenever a preacher or a teacher teaches a scripture in a sermon or class that I don't understand—[Mom would then pause and one hand would slap the other]—I go after it! I go home and get out every version of the Bible that I have and read that passage. I get out the Hebrew or the Greek dictionary to help me find the true meanings of the words. I study the comments of scholars on that passage, so that by the end of the day I have a pretty good handle on what the scripture really means." Now that, my friends, is a true Bible student and a Pearl Seeker.

Read Ephesians 5:8–21. Make your own list of how to walk as a child of Light.

____

____

____

____

____

____

In Ephesians 5:8 Paul urged the Christians at Ephesus to walk as children of Light. God means for His children to walk confidently in their faith and in their knowledge of who God is.

- Do we know all the ins and outs of the Light?
- Do we know our instruction book, the Bible, through and through?
- Have we sat for hours and days on end, studying the truth that Jesus, the Son of God, brought down to earth?

- Do we let our minds dwell on an eternity with God or on an eternity with Satan?
- Do we attend gospel meetings and lectureships and seminars that enable us to sit at the feet of some of the finest Christian minds in our generation?
- Do we even know how to teach the gospel that will save men's souls?
- Can we reach out to a lost world with biblical passages that will bring comfort to humanity and convert them?
- Do we make a difference and stand for the Light and right?
- Do we have the scriptures in our heads to heal someone's broken heart?
- Do we even care to know what plan God has in store for us here?
- Do we know Him?
- Do we just know?

CALLED TO A SECOND CHANCE IN LEARNING

Jesus called us to learn from Him by yoking up with Him:

> Come to Me, all who are weary and heavy-laden, and I will give you rest. Take My yoke upon you and learn from Me, for I am gentle and humble in heart, and you will find rest for your souls. For My yoke is easy and My burden is light (Matthew 11:28–30).

Jesus still calls across the ages to all of us, beckoning, "Learn *from* Me." The King James Version says, "Learn *of* me." How am I going to learn from Jesus and how am I going to learn of Jesus? There is only one place where I can learn, and that is the Bible.

Paul urged the Colossian church to follow a list of attributes essential for the Christian walk:

> We have not ceased to pray for you and to ask that you may be filled with the knowledge of His will in all spiritual wisdom and understanding, so that you may walk in a manner worthy of the Lord, to please Him in all respects, bearing fruit in every good work and increasing in the knowledge of God (Colossians 1:9–10).

Knowledge is mentioned twice in these two verses. Paul's desire was for the church to be filled with the knowledge of God's will for them, but he also wanted them to increase, to grow in themselves the knowledge of God. God has always wanted His people to know more about Him. That will never change. Wisdom and understanding enable us to walk worthy of the Lord.

In Isaiah 2 we see the Messianic prophet prophesying about the church that would be established in Jerusalem on the day of Pentecost. "And many peoples will come and say, 'Come, let us go up to the mountain of the Lord, to the house of the God of Jacob; that He may teach us concerning His ways, and that we may walk in His paths'" (Isaiah 2:3).

Who will teach us? God will teach us everything we need to know. He has not failed us yet. Again, this teaching enables us to walk in His paths.

DIG AND LEARN FOR THE DESIRES OF YOUR HEART

The more I study the Bible, the more I realize how much I do not know! There is so much to learn, to ponder, and to discover, and I will never know it all. That treasure chest I call the Bible beckons all of us to gather around and listen and dig and learn. Will we set our hearts on this marvelous gift from God? Will we be like that skilled scribe Ezra and make up our minds to learn? Will we, as David did, say to God again and again, "Teach me Your statutes"? (Psalm 119:26). Becoming a Bible student is where the Pearl Seeker begins.

Ezra was a great leader and priest. He taught Israel the truth. His task certainly was not easy, but the Lord was with him.

Can we, too, be like Ezra and set our minds on the Lord? Oh, yes! God inspired Paul to write: "If then you have been raised up with Christ, keep seeking the things above, where Christ is, seated at the right hand of God. Set your mind on the things above, not on the things that are on earth" (Colossians 3:1–2).

As we end this chapter, I must share one more passage that fits so aptly here. Psalm 37:4 says, "Delight yourself in the Lord; and He will give you the desires of your heart."

Delight yourself in His Word, His commandments, His truth. When you are seeking the face of God, the Father will bless you over and over. He will give you the desires of your heart—even the dreams that you thought would never come true.

Psalm 37:4 describes Ezra. He delighted in God. And the good hand of his God was upon him. Ezra made up his mind to know everything there was to know about Jehovah God, and God blessed Ezra for that. Ezra also made the decision to live and teach nothing but Jehovah God. It was the best decision he ever made.

Prayer: Lord, help me to seek second chances!

Song: Nearer, Still Nearer

Nearer, still nearer, close to Thy heart,
Draw me, my Savior—so precious Thou art!
Fold me, oh, fold me close to Thy breast;
Shelter me safe in that "haven of rest";
Shelter me safe in that "haven of rest."

Nearer, still nearer, nothing I bring,
Naught as an off'ring to Jesus, my King;
Only my sinful, now contrite heart,
Grant me the cleansing Thy blood doth impart;
Grant me the cleansing Thy blood doth impart.

Nearer, still nearer, Lord, to be Thine!
Sin, with its follies, I gladly resign,
All of its pleasures, pomp and its pride,
Give me but Jesus, my Lord crucified;
Give me but Jesus, my Lord crucified.

Nearer, still nearer, while life shall last,
Till safe in glory my anchor is cast;
Through endless ages ever to be
Nearer, my Savior, still nearer to Thee;
Nearer, my Savior, still nearer to Thee!

Digging for Pearls

1. Describe how far Israel had fallen from God.

2. Did God forgive Israel?

3. How important is it for Christians to read the Bible daily?

4. How might Isaiah 55:6 imply that there is a time when the Lord may not be found or may not be near?

   "Seek the Lord while He may be found; Call upon Him while He is near" (Isaiah 55:6).

5. Explain what this passage means to you: "The grass withers, the flower fades, but the word of our God stands forever" (Isaiah 40:8).

Pearl Drop

Know Before Whom You Stand!

Have you ever visited the Holocaust Museum in Washington, DC, or perhaps in another city? Put it on your "bucket list." I feel that everyone needs to walk through its rooms and listen to the personal stories. A warning here: It is definitely not for young children; this museum is for adults.

Our family loves history and museums, so upon arriving in Washington years ago on spring break, we headed off to this particular museum. Upon entering we were given a passport book which contained a small biography of someone who had experienced firsthand the horror of Hitler's Nazi Germany. The men in our tour group were given passports of men, and we women were given passports of women. We were to be that person who walked the steps of this unbelievable persecution.

When our tour group gathered in the elevator, I opened my passport and promptly gasped. The woman of my passport had the same name as I, Rebecca, and we both were born in March. The tour guide asked, "Are you all right?"

"No, not exactly," I replied. Then I showed him my passport and informed him of the uncanny similarities.

He nodded and said, "Then your journey will be more meaningful."

We began our journey going through rooms containing newspapers and actual videos telling the unbelievable story of Hitler's rise to power. Then we entered a room that displayed a railroad car, a replica of the rail system used to transfer the millions of Jews to the labor camps such as Auschwitz and Birkenau. Another room, extremely disturbing, was filled with nothing but shoes, suitcases, and more shoes. And the smell

of shoes! Actual shoes of men, women, and children who had made a long one-way journey into the darkness of tyranny. A long hall displayed pictures from floor to ceiling of people and families who once made up European villages. But these people were Jews who were seized and taken away from their homes. Their villages no longer exist. All the people are gone. There are no words to describe the feeling.

But there is one more room that I must tell you about. It is a very large room which chronicled "Kristallnacht"—the night when Nazi Germany attacked Jews in Germany and Austria in 1938. *Kristallnacht* means the "night of broken glass," as it refers to the shards of glass that covered the streets due to the destruction of synagogues and Jewish-owned businesses. More than a thousand synagogues were burned and obliterated.

Also in this room was a very intriguing piece of wood that resembled a huge mantelpiece. It was surrounded by plexiglass so no one could touch it. This large framework once covered the entrance to the cabinet that held the Torah—the Law, the first five books of the Old Testament—in a synagogue. The Nazis had tried to destroy the mantel. Numerous ax marks were evidence. Some Hebrew words were solemnly and heavily inscribed in this mantel—words that even Hitler could not destroy. What did these words mean? A small sign displayed beside the plexiglass gave me the information I was searching for. The Hebrew words said: "Know before Whom you stand."

Here was a sober admonition for the Jewish rabbi or priest of that particular synagogue to remember always that he stood before God as he handled and read the first five books of the Bible. Isn't this very similar to the times God told Moses and also Joshua to remove their sandals because they were standing on holy ground? (Exodus 3, Joshua 5).

What is the lesson for us? There are so many! But the main one is that we, too, need to know before Whom we stand. How important it is for us to understand the enormity of being in the presence of God as we read and handle His powerful Word! We stand before Jehovah God, the Almighty God, El Shaddai, El Adonai, Yahweh every time we open the

Bible! Across the pages of His magnificent book our Creator opens His mouth and personally speaks to each of us. He has a life-changing message to tell, and who will listen? Do we grasp the concept of the Father, the Son, and the Holy Spirit being with us as we worship every Sunday? This is serious business, as we realize we too are on holy ground.

We are accustomed to bringing everything down to our level and dumbing our society to the point that we have diluted our Father in heaven, too. Our casual society approaches Him with, "Hey there, Dad," in an attempt to reduce Him to the man on the street! He is God, not man. He is the great I AM.

How many Christians really know God—who He is and what He says to us in the Bible? Once again, it is Pearl Seekers, the men and women who make it a practice to dig deeply into the Word and have a relationship with Him through prayer, that know who our God is. Knowledge does not come through some kind of spiritual osmosis. It comes through hard work and the desire to please the Father.

Listen to God as He speaks through Solomon:

> My son, if you will receive My words and treasure My commandments within you, make your ear attentive to wisdom, incline your heart to understanding; for if you cry for discernment, lift your voice for understanding; if you seek her as silver and search for her as for hidden treasures; then you will discern the fear of the Lord and discover the knowledge of God. For the Lord gives wisdom; from His mouth come knowledge and understanding (Proverbs 2:1–6).

God the Father, God the Son, and God the Holy Spirit kindly beckon us to sit at their feet and learn. The question is, will we get our selfish selves out of the way and take the time? Will we make God the top priority in our lives?

Look at the kindness of God in Isaiah 1:18: "Come now, and let us reason together." God never force feeds us or orders us: *Sit down; hush now; be quiet; you had better listen to Me and learn!* Instead He invites us to the feast that will last forever. He is reasonable, and what He asks of us is reasonable.

Know before whom you stand, my sisters. Have reverence and awe and bless His holy name, for God is good.

> Shout joyfully to the Lord, all the earth. Serve the Lord with gladness; come before Him with joyful singing. Know that the Lord Himself is God; it is He who has made us, and not we ourselves; we are His people and the sheep of His pasture. Enter His gates with thanksgiving and His courts with praise. Give thanks to Him, bless His name. For the Lord is good; His lovingkindness is everlasting and His faithfulness to all generations (Psalm 100).

CHAPTER 6

Seek To Be Just a Christian

My people are destroyed for lack of knowledge. Because you have rejected knowledge, I also will reject you from being My priest. Since you have forgotten the law of your God, I also will forget your children (Hosea 4:6).

JUST A CHRISTIAN

Are you a Christian? Do you wear the name of Jesus Christ? Being a Christian is the biggest blessing you and I will ever know. Just think about it. In the whole scheme of things God has seen fit to let you hear the gospel of Jesus Christ. Some will stand before the Judgment Seat of the Lord and say, "I never heard your gospel, Lord." But that will not be you—or me.

Some of you were raised in Christian homes. Not everyone has that privilege, do they? We ought to get down on our knees every day and thank God for that privilege alone! Perhaps it wasn't the best Christian home, but at least there were some Christian values taught there. To be raised by Christian parents who lead the way is God's plan for every child, but you and I know two things. Not all parents are Christians, and not all Christian parents set the right examples.

"Why is that?" you ask. Well, God has given man the freedom of making his own choices. Many people believe in God but don't believe God! God doesn't grab us by the hand, march us down the church aisle, and hold us forcefully under the waters of baptism until we shout, "I believe!" God never forces anyone to grow in the faith or study the Bible or pray daily. He never causes anyone to be faithful. These are decisions made on our part.

DONKEY YEARS

Young people don't always make the best of choices. Mom used to say that we make some of the most important decisions of our lives in our donkey years when we are immature and acting foolishly. We decide who to marry, what occupation to pursue, and where to live when we are young, immature, and not so wise. If we are faithful to the Lord, He will show us how to live, where to live, and with whom to share our lives.

God's plan is for us to seek Him, but that is not always our choice. Sometimes we just don't listen, and we don't desire to be better. We are too busy for spiritual matters. We don't have time for God or for attending church. We have other things on our agendas: work, promotions, new house, vacations, to name a few.

It is very easy to become parents whose priorities are not in the right order. Then the entire family suffers because immature Christians are leading that family. What a price these parents and children will pay in the long run! By the time most parents wake up to the importance of what God has to say, the children are grown up and having their own say. Precious souls are at stake here.

SHIFT TO THE SIMPLE CALL

However, that does not have to be the case. There are many Christian families who have turned themselves around just in time, and their focus has shifted to God and His plan for them. Many parents hearken to that wake-up call, see the light at the end of the tunnel, and ask God to rescue them from Satan's grasp. How marvelous it is to realize that once again our God of second chances makes it simple for families to begin again! The blessing here is that God loves His children, and as our concerned Father, He continues to alert us and rescue us from foolish decisions.

Here is a key verse for Christians of all ages:

> See how great a love the Father has bestowed on us, that we would be called children of God; and such we are. For this reason the world does not know us, because it did not know Him (1 John 3:1).

God looks at Christians as His children—His sons and His daughters. That is almost too wonderful. We are His family, and He is our loving Father. Surely one of the reasons God created the family concept of father and child was so we could understand Him as our Father when we become a Christian—His child. For those of us who are parents and know personally the deep, abiding love we have for our own children, we are simply overwhelmed as we realize the indescribable love God has for us. That is hard to grasp. Why has God done so much for us?

HIS WAY FOR ME

Notice that John describes the love God has for His children as great. And it is great! Look at your own life: what the Father has done for you, what He is doing for you, and what He will do for you. This is a faith builder if there ever was one!

I struggled with God before I obeyed the gospel in baptism. I was old enough, and I knew what God wanted of me. I knew the scriptures and the examples of baptism in the Bible backward and forward. I truly wanted to be baptized, but I balked at it. I just kept procrastinating. I knew my parents were very concerned about me, but I could not seem to take the final step. It was summertime, and I was twelve-and-a-half. My two siblings had been immersed when they were younger than I was, and I know my hesitation bothered them too.

But still I resisted. Dad was the preacher, and when he led the invitation hymn, I stood and sang with everyone else, but I refused to look at him. I was too embarrassed and ashamed.

Finally, one Sunday morning, we were all getting ready to go downstairs in our home in Concord where the church was meeting. I walked into the kitchen where Mom was waiting, ready to walk down the steps to our basement. I will never forget that moment as long as I live. She turned to me and simply said, "Becky, you don't love Jesus."

"Don't love Jesus?" I replied. "Of course I love Jesus!" I was horrified.

Mom said softly, "No, you don't. Because Jesus said, 'If you love me, you will keep my commandments.'" She then turned and walked downstairs.

That was it. That was all my mother needed to say. I knew what she was conveying. I loved the Lord and it was time to show how much. It was time to step over the line.

That day I repented of my sins and confessed the name of Jesus, my Savior. Dad baptized me in the cool Blackwater River of New Hampshire. I became a Christian. I have never felt so wonderful. As I write now, I still remember the feeling of going under the water and coming up from the grave—forgiven. How beautiful to begin again! It was a happy day.

Sisters, baptism is humbling, and for many it is a stumbling block. It was for me. It is hard to submit to the act of being immersed in water, because it is surrendering to God. But we must remember, baptism is God's plan, not ours. That is God's way, not ours. He knows what He is doing and what He is asking.

NAAMAN BALKED AT SIMPLICITY

There is a baptism story in 2 Kings 5. When the leprous captain of the Syrian army was told by Elisha to go and dip seven times in the Jordan River, Naaman balked. He did not like the manner or the method of the truth Elisha imparted to him. He did not want to do the very thing that would restore his life. And on top of that, Naaman had an attitude problem. Let's read about it:

> But Naaman was furious and went away and said, "Behold, I thought, 'He will surely come out to me and stand and call on the name of the Lord his God, and wave his hand over the place and cure the leper.' Are not Abanah and Pharpar, the rivers of Damascus, better than all the waters of Israel? Could I not wash in them and be clean?"

> So he turned and went away in a rage. Then his servants came near and spoke to him and said, "My father, had the prophet told you to do some great thing, would you not have done it? How much more then, when he says to you, 'Wash, and be clean'?" So he went down and dipped himself seven times in the Jordan, according to the word of the man of God; and his flesh was restored like the flesh of a little child and he was clean (2 Kings 5:11–14).

Naaman was angry because of Elisha's words, but he had a good relationship with his servants. Otherwise, he would not have listened to their words. He saw that his servants were right and he was wrong. This was not a time for pride to stand in the way of healing. Naaman also realized it was not about him, but it was about obedience, submission, and immersion. (That too must have been difficult for the Syrian captain.) He had the chance of a lifetime for a miracle, and he knew he did not have the luxury of wasting one more second with the deadly leprosy slowly eating his life away. Time was of the essence. It was a matter of life and death—his life and his death.

Naaman surrendered and went down into the water and immersed himself seven times. When he came back up the seventh time, God had stepped in and delivered Naaman. He no longer had the dreaded disease.

Naaman had to submit to God, and so do we. When I was twelve-and-a-half, God stepped in and delivered Becky. I learned that submission and obedience to God are the only way to live. True happiness comes when you don't fight God!

LOOK! WATER!

After the Ethiopian eunuch listened to Philip's teaching of the gospel in Acts 8, what did he do? He had the option of obeying the gospel and being saved or riding off into the sunset as lost as lost could be.

> Then Philip opened his mouth, and beginning from this Scripture he preached Jesus to him. As they went along the road they came to some water; and the eunuch said, "Look! Water! What prevents me from being baptized?" And Philip said, "If you believe with all your

> heart, you may." And he answered and said, "I believe that Jesus Christ is the Son of God." And he ordered the chariot to stop; and they both went down into the water, Philip as well as the eunuch, and he baptized him. When they came up out of the water, the Spirit of the Lord snatched Philip away; and the eunuch no longer saw him, but went on his way rejoicing (Acts 8:35–39).

The Ethiopian eunuch was quite a man! He had no problem with authority or submission. He heard the gospel and obeyed it. He had a wonderful heart, ready and willing to obey. And don't you love the last verse which tells us how the eunuch traveled back home to Ethiopia—rejoicing! Did baptism bring sorrow, doom, and gloom? Absolutely not. Just the opposite. Obeying God's commandments brings joy and happiness and peace—every time.

Let's go back to the beginning of the Christian walk. When a person is baptized into Christ and comes up from the watery grave, there is so much to rejoice about! That person is clean, washed in the blood of our Savior Jesus. Her sins have been forgiven and washed away; she is a new woman. And she gets to start her life anew, walking with her Father, her Savior, and her Comforter. All three of them are involved in her life, helping as she takes her baby steps of the Christian walk. As she grows and matures in the faith, the Godhead is still there by her side, delivering her, helping her, and maturing her because she is precious to them. She is a child of the King—she has a place in the family. She is loved. Her prayers are heard. What blessings are poured on her head!

> Therefore we have been buried with Him through baptism into death, so that as Christ was raised from the dead through the glory of the Father, so we too might walk in newness of life (Romans 6:4).

OBEDIENCE: FATHER IS WELL-PLEASED

This new walk with the Lord is surely a reason to rejoice and rejoice. Paul was inspired to write what I call the double whammy verse—a verse that repeats itself: "Rejoice in the Lord always; again I will say, rejoice!" (Philippians 4:4).

When Jesus was baptized by John (Matthew 3), we see a rare scene. We observe the presence of the Trinity—the Father, the Son, and the Holy Spirit. Let's read it:

> After being baptized, Jesus came up immediately from the water; and behold, the heavens were opened, and He saw the Spirit of God descending as a dove and lighting on Him, and behold, a voice out of the heavens said, "This is My beloved Son, in whom I am well-pleased" (Matthew 3:16–17).

What a sight! Jesus comes up out of the baptismal waters of the Jordan; the Holy Spirit descends from heaven as a dove, lighting on Jesus; and the Father's voice announces these precious, all confirming words: "This is My beloved Son, in whom I am well-pleased."

When the Bible was written, there were no chapter-and-verse divisions. They were added to help students find passages. Let's read the first verse of chapter 4 as it really is, right after verse 17: "Then Jesus was led up by the Spirit into the wilderness to be tempted by the devil."

It's interesting to note that immediately—not months later, but immediately—Jesus prepared Himself for the monstrous temptation by Satan in the wilderness. We know that Jesus was perfect and had no sin, but is it just a coincidence that He suffered a huge temptation from the devil soon after He was immersed? I believe there is a definite parallel here. After we are baptized, we become Satan's new project. He tempts us to sin by dangling immorality and worthless treasures before our eyes continually, setting all kinds of traps for us.

I'M NOT ALONE

Is there no hope for the new Christian, or any Christian, for that matter? Has God abandoned us? Listen, my sisters, God is our marvelous Father who loves us and helps us in all situations. He has not left us alone to fend for ourselves.

Listen to one of my favorite scriptures in the whole Bible: "You are from God, little children, and have overcome them; because greater is

He who is in you than he who is in the world" (1 John 4:4). Now notice what Paul said to the Corinthians:

> No temptation has overtaken you but such as is common to man; and God is faithful, who will not allow you to be tempted beyond what you are able, but with the temptation will provide the way of escape also, so that you will be able to endure it (1 Corinthians 10:13).

Our God is bigger and better than Satan. If you are a Christian, God is in you, helping you to overcome every trick and trap Satan sets for you. God beats Satan every time! Also, the Father knows what Satan is trying to pull on us, so He has given us an escape route. What comfort these passages are, and what faith builders they are!

God's plan from the very beginning involved you and me. He knew that Jesus was going to come to earth even before sin entered the garden. God knows all things—He is omniscient. God is everywhere all the time—He is omnipresent. And God is all-powerful and can do anything He chooses to do—He is omnipotent. Do a study of Psalm 139 and see what an eye opener this is for every Christian.

DEATHBLOW TO SATAN

God knew that Jesus would be born in the little town of Bethlehem, that His ministry would begin when He was about thirty, and that He would die for the sins of the world. Jesus and the Holy Spirit knew these things, too. God knew that Satan would attack His Son, but Jesus dealt Satan a deathblow when He conquered death and rose on the third day.

> And I will put enmity between you and the woman, and between your seed and her seed; He shall bruise you on the head, and you shall bruise Him on the heel (Genesis 3:15).

From Genesis to Revelation, we encounter the Satan factor. We see the devil trying to wreak havoc in the lives of those who love God. From the garden of Eden to our living rooms, Satan roams the earth, looking for innocent victims he can completely consume. He is not interested in a little nibble here or a little nibble there. He wants to eat us up completely! God gives us a graphic description of Satan:

> Be of sober spirit, be on the alert. Your adversary, the devil, prowls around like a roaring lion, seeking someone to devour. But resist him, firm in your faith, knowing that the same experiences of suffering are being accomplished by your brethren who are in the world (1 Peter 5:8–9).

Have you ever wondered why Satan has such wrath? Why is he so angry? Maybe he is angry because he knows he will never get a second chance to repent. He has been judged and condemned by God the Creator. That prophecy pronounced in Eden was fulfilled by the events at the cross and the empty tomb. He and his demons are doomed to hell for all eternity, and there will be no forgiveness for them. On the other hand, Satan sees how you and I receive forgiveness again and again. He sees how we can be restored to a loving relationship with the Father—something he will never have. He sees our forgiving God with His arms outstretched to prodigal daughters and faithful daughters, and that makes the devil venomous, toxic, and deadly. He knows there is absolutely no hope for him. What Satan once had in heaven will never again be his. Therefore, Satan prowls about, looking for ways to steal us away from God, to tempt us to sin, to blacken our pure hearts, and to wholly consume us. How smug Satan must feel when he is able to steal a Christian from the fold.

CHOICE: SIMPLE, NOT EASY

Remember, my friends, we choose to yield to temptation. God has always given man freedom of choice. Sin is alluring because most of us see only Satan's bait, never his hook. And before we know it, we are caught up in more sins, lies, addictive lifestyles—the list goes on and on. Here is a passage that disturbs me.

> This is the judgment, that the Light has come into the world, and men loved the darkness rather than the Light, for their deeds were evil. For everyone who does evil hates the Light, and does not come

> to the Light for fear that his deeds will be exposed. But he who practices the truth comes to the Light, so that his deeds may be manifested as having been wrought in God (John 3:19–21).

How interesting it is to note that Jesus, the Light, came into the world, but men *loved* the darkness, not the Light. This passage does not say that men liked the darkness, but "men loved the darkness." Why? Because they loved doing wrong! They did not want to embrace Christ, the Light, the Right. Man in general does not want to get rid of his sinful ways. He really hates change! How true that is! Satan has made sin seem like so much fun that the world refuses to let it go. It is true, isn't it, that men and women loved the darkness then, and they love the darkness now?

John, the beloved apostle, was inspired by the Holy Spirit to write this about Satan: "We know that we are of God, and that the whole world lies in the power of the evil one" (1 John 5:19). That is still true today, isn't it? Nothing has changed. The entire world still lies in the power of Satan. But Jesus still came.

Not all of mankind would choose to be saved. Not all would want to know Jesus. But Jesus still came. Not all Christians will stay true to the Master. But Jesus still came and died.

It is very important for everyone to realize that God does not look down from heaven, deciding who will be saved and who will be lost. He never plays that children's game—Eeny, Meeny, Miny, Moe—to choose someone to love Him. That part is up to us. The truth of the matter is that God does not want anyone to be lost. Peter wrote: "The Lord is not slow about His promise, as some count slowness, but is patient toward you, not wishing for any to perish but for all to come to repentance" (2 Peter 3:9). But we realistically know that not everyone will choose to love God or serve Him.

THE SIMPLE GOSPEL

Fifty days after Jesus' resurrection, the Jews celebrated Pentecost. Many of those who made the annual trip to Jerusalem to celebrate the Passover stayed those fifty days and celebrated Pentecost before returning home.

Read Acts 2 and see the apostles being filled with the Holy Spirit and speaking to the Jews gathered from every nation under heaven. There's no way we can know the exact number in that audience who witnessed the miracles of that day. The city of Jerusalem was definitely swollen with visitors. One Bible historian guessed that more than 2,000,000 were in the city. Another suggested 250,000. Even if ten percent of the Jews came to the gathering, you can deduce that thousands of souls crowded to hear Peter preach the first gospel sermon:

> "Therefore let all the house of Israel know for certain that God has made Him both Lord and Christ—this Jesus whom you crucified." Now when they heard this, they were pierced to the heart, and said to Peter and the rest of the apostles, "Brethren, what shall we do?" Peter said to them, "Repent, and each of you be baptized in the name of Jesus Christ for the forgiveness of your sins; and you will receive the gift of the Holy Spirit. For the promise is for you and your children and for all who are far off, as many as the Lord our God will call to Himself." And with many other words he solemnly testified and kept on exhorting them, saying, "Be saved from this perverse generation!" So then, those who had received his word were baptized; and that day there were added about three thousand souls. They were continually devoting themselves to the apostles' teaching and to fellowship, to the breaking of bread and to prayer (Acts 2:36–42).

A NEW WAY: SIMPLE AND BETTER

Peter preached; hearts were touched; men and women were baptized; the church began. The day of Pentecost was ground zero for the church. The new covenant was born. About three thousand souls were added to the number that day, and more were to come the next day and the next, as the gospel spread like wildfire. These were the very first New Testament Christians. What zeal and fervor they had as they returned to their native countries and taught others the good news of Jesus Christ! Even when Rome's persecution and hostilities abounded, the Word of God would not be silenced. Why not? Because it was the Word of God, and no one can silence God! Rome's every effort to squelch Christianity backfired. The attempts to rid the world of Christ and His teaching only added fuel to the fire.

The moment for Christianity had arrived. It was time for Christianity to change the world, and it certainly did. The world has never been the same since Jesus came and fulfilled His mission to seek and save the lost (Luke 19:10).

Although Jesus is no longer on earth, His mission goes on today. Millions of hearts who crave forgiveness of sins, peace, and salvation still want to do what God calls them to do. People still respond to Jesus' cry in John 10:10: "I came that they may have life, and have it abundantly." Who doesn't want forgiveness, the chance to start over, and then receive the abundant life? I surely do! And so did many on Pentecost.

The Christian life is the abundant life! I am rejoicing every day because the Scriptures tell us: "But God demonstrates His own love toward us, in that while we were yet sinners, Christ died for us" (Romans 5:8).

CHOSEN FOR MERCY AND GRACE

God didn't wait for Becky to get her act together before He sent Jesus to die. He did not postpone Christ's coming because the Pharisees were such hypocrites. He didn't stop because some were too focused on pleasure to notice they were lost. But God sent Jesus even when He knew you and I would later be born and grow up to become sinners, dumb kids doing dumb things. Jesus still came.

Peter was inspired to say to these first Christians and to us today:

> But you are a chosen race, a royal priesthood, a holy nation, a people for God's own possession, so that you may proclaim the excellencies of Him who has called you out of darkness into His marvelous light; for you once were not a people, but now you are the people of God; you had not received mercy, but now you have received mercy (1 Peter 2:9–10).

Me—a chosen race? You—a royal priesthood? We—a holy nation? How can these things be? When you hear the gospel call, you have two choices: obey it or reject it. If you obey it, you become part of the family of God, and you receive mercy. Mercy? What is mercy? Compassion; lovingkindness. Do you want it? Do I want it? Sure do. I want every bit of it because I am human; I make many mistakes. I am a sinner, and Jesus died for sinners like me. Listen to how Paul put it:

> And you were dead in your trespasses and sins, in which you formerly walked according to the course of this world, according to the prince of the power of the air, of the spirit that is now working in the sons of disobedience. Among them we too all formerly lived in the lusts of our flesh, indulging the desires of the flesh and of the mind, and were by nature children of wrath, even as the rest. But God, being rich in mercy, because of His great love with which He loved us, even when we were dead in our transgressions, made us alive together with Christ (by grace you have been saved), and raised us up with Him, and seated us with Him in the heavenly places in Christ Jesus, so that in the ages to come He might show the surpassing riches of His grace in kindness toward us in Christ Jesus. For by grace you have been saved through faith; and that not of yourselves, it is the gift of God; not as a result of works, so that no one may boast. For we are His workmanship, created in Christ Jesus for good works, which God prepared beforehand so that we would walk in them (Ephesians 2:1–10).

When I look at this entire section of scripture, the words that jump out at me are these: *being rich in mercy.* Who was so rich in mercy? Our heavenly Father was. Even though we were children of wrath and full of sin, God still loved us and sent His Son to die for us. I don't know if I really can get my mind wrapped around that one, but what I do understand is that my Father loves me—why, I don't know—and has mercy on me. Mercy. Compassion and lovingkindness on me. I want mercy, girls, not justice, and our God is rich in mercy, not poor in mercy. There is plenty to go around.

Three times in these verses, *grace* is used. What is grace? We always say that grace is God's unmerited favor. The gift of grace is from God because there is nothing we could possibly do or say that would earn our salvation. We will never be worthy of Jesus' sacrifice on the old rugged cross. Even if you and I spent every minute of every day working and serving the Lord for the rest of our lives, our works would not merit the forgiveness of one sin, to say nothing of the salvation God offers so freely. Verse 7 expresses it so beautifully as "the surpassing riches of His grace." Once again, God is rich towards us.

Some say grace is God's unmerited favor. Some say grace is God's richness at Christ's expense. Some say grace is free, but it's not cheap. Some say grace is when God is better to us than we deserve. Everyone who has received grace will say that God's grace is amazing. But don't forget, grace is also a great teacher. Grace teaches us how we should not live—that we should deny ungodliness and worldly lusts. Grace also teaches us how we should live—that we should live soberly, righteously, and godly in this world. When we learn grace, we will be more gracious to others, we will live in grace, and we will glorify God because of His grace. May God help us to learn from His amazing grace!

—Jeff Jenkins' blog, August 14, 2015

Read Ephesians 2:1–10 again. What a marvelous passage! Paul explains what God has done for all those who have left the world's path and chosen to walk with Jesus! Note Paul's words *we* and *all*, as Paul identifies himself as a sinner, too, who used to be dead in his sins but now is alive because of Christ. But because of God's love for all of us and being so rich in His grace and mercy, we also are no longer dead but alive. All this is the gift of God.

THE HUMAN FACTOR

So I ask you. Why doesn't everyone want to be just a Christian? Why can't it be just that simple? This life is so full of troubles, highs and lows, problems, sorrows, stresses, and challenges. Who wants to walk through these difficult times alone? Mental institutions are full of people who cannot handle the stress of daily living, people who feel guilty and hopeless.

I have been to many funeral homes to comfort grieving families. I have grieved there myself when my parents and sister passed away. I could never have made it through those difficult times without my Father, His Son, and His Spirit. Their comfort and presence were just what I needed, as they soothed my soul.

Have you ever had a health crisis? Have you heard a doctor say, "You have cancer"? Have you sat with a loved one who heard that diagnosis? Have you wrapped your arms around a sister or brother who has a terminal illness and wept with them?

We Christians often ask, "What do people do who don't have God in their lives? How do they get through this?" I don't know how they get through those times. I don't want to know. I am thankful to be just a Christian and belong to God!

Through the years there have been multiple occasions when I watched a Christian brother or sister walk through the valley of the shadow with God. I have seen all kinds of tragedy: the sudden deaths of children, all kinds of cancers and diseases, infidelities of a spouse, sexual abuse, adultery, bankruptcies, pedophilia, alcoholism, and homosexuality. Yes, Solomon surely spoke the truth when he said repeatedly in Ecclesiastes, "There is nothing new under the sun." My mother used to say, "Honey, if you live long enough, you will see just about everything in the church."

We must never be shocked when tragedies occur or when brethren fall into temptation's grasp. The Satan factor is real and alive. We all sin (Romans 3:23). Christians are not immune. Satan will try everything in his clever bag of tricks to reel us in. Even then, our kind, gracious, and merciful Father will "provide the way of escape" so that we can endure temptation (1 Corinthians 10:13).

Satan wants us to give up all hope. His desire is for God's children to constantly feel unworthy, unloved, negative, and depressed. He will stop at nothing to keep us out of the most marvelous book ever written—the precious Bible. Satan knows that the answers to all our questions are there.

But God's desire is for us to know Him and to love Him! Look at Philippians 1:9: "And this I pray, that your love may abound still more and more in real knowledge and all discernment."

CHRISTIANITY SIMPLY TAKES TIME

We cannot become a Christian and stay neutral and idle. We have many jobs to do, and one of those jobs is to grow, grow, grow in the knowledge of God. Listen girls, we are either growing in the faith or we are dying on the vine!

Take time for the Lord every day. Make an appointment to meet with Him every day to read His Word and to talk to Him in prayer. Then you will be walking with the Master.

Remember, girls, God knows our hearts and minds. We don't fool Him. He knows whether we truly love Him or not. Look at these interesting passages describing God's intimate knowledge of us:

> O Lord, You have searched me and known me (Psalm 139:1).

> Would not God find this out? For He knows the secrets of the heart (Psalm 44:21).

> But You know me, O Lord; You see me; and You examine my heart's attitude toward You (Jeremiah 12:3).

> I the Lord search the heart, I test the mind, even to give to each man according to his ways, according to the results of his deeds (Jeremiah 17:10).

> And He who searches the hearts knows what the mind of the Spirit is, because He intercedes for the saints according to the will of God (Romans 8:27).

I am thankful that God knows all there is to know about us. His omniscient mind is unfathomable and inscrutable. Only God can understand God. Yet I am so thankful that He is in charge of all things, especially your life and my life.

I NEED THE LORD

I am so thankful that our God is in charge and He reigns! To be His child is the best, because when we wear Jesus' blood, we get another chance. God knows what we are; He made us. And He forgives. He will go right on loving us and maintaining a close relationship with us, if we make things right with Him.

> But if we walk in the Light as He Himself is in the Light, we have fellowship with one another, and the blood of Jesus His Son cleanses us from all sin. If we say that we have no sin, we are deceiving ourselves and the truth is not in us. If we confess our sins, He is faithful and righteous to forgive us our sins and to cleanse us from all unrighteousness (1 John 1:7–9).

> Our God reigns. When we feel uncomfortable with what is going on in the world, our God reigns. When we are uncertain about the future, our God reigns. When we are weak, our God reigns. When we have been disappointed or feel forsaken by others, our God reigns. When we are struggling with sadness, loss, or loneliness, our God reigns. When we feel like our world is falling apart, our God reigns. Praise God, He is still on His throne. Our God reigns!
>
> —Jeff Jenkins blog, January 31, 2015

My sisters, we need the Lord desperately. I know that I do! I can tell Him anything on my heart, and He hears me. He is guiding me on this Christian journey, and He will never forsake me. He hears my cries, my begging prayers, my fears. He knows my concerns, my stresses, and my trials. And when I pray, I believe my loving Savior stands beside me and intercedes, "My Father, I know what she is trying to say. I know what she is going through. I have been there."

> Therefore, since we have a great high priest who has passed through the heavens, Jesus the Son of God, let us hold fast our confession.

> For we do not have a high priest who cannot sympathize with our weaknesses, but One who has been tempted in all things as we are, yet without sin. Therefore let us draw near with confidence to the throne of grace, so that we may receive mercy and find grace to help in time of need (Hebrews 4:14–16).

What a blessing to have the Son of God interceding for me! I am able to fall on my knees before the Father's throne of grace. And what is the result? I find mercy and grace to help me. All I can say is, *What in the world did I ever do to deserve all this? All I ever did was choose to love Him and obey Him. It is too wonderful for me to grasp, but I am just so grateful for it. I will thank Him every day for loving me.*

How thankful I am to have a Father who has put me into His family, called me His daughter, wrapped His arms around me, and says to me daily: "I am your Father, and you are mine."

And I say once more, "Why doesn't everybody want mercy? Why doesn't everybody want God's marvelous grace? Why doesn't everybody want forgiveness? Why doesn't everybody want to go to heaven?"

Why oh why doesn't everybody want to be just a Christian?

Prayer: Lord, help me to be just a Christian.

Song: I Love the Lord

I love the Lord, for He died my soul to save.
On Calvary, His dear life He freely gave;
From realms above, Jesus feely came to die,
That I might live someday with Him on High.

Chorus:
I love the Lord, He has been so good to me.
He gave His life, from sin to set me free,
No greater love than His could ever be,
I love the Lord, because He first loved me.

I love the Lord, for He saved the lost from sin,
He gave them life to be whole and free again;
To live on high, with Him nevermore to die,
Oh, praise His name, we'll see Him by and by.

I love the Lord, for His love so full and free,
He taught us why that our love like His should be;
To be like Him, and compassion freely give,
Oh, bless His name, we then with Him could live.

Digging for Pearls

1. How is it a blessing to hear the gospel of Jesus?

2. Why is baptism a stumbling block for many?

3. Why is Satan so angry?

Pearl Drop

The Crying Man

I can still see his face in my memory. He was a tall, husky man, cowboy-like in appearance, one who was accustomed to working outdoors. He wore a plaid shirt and a pair of jeans. He was fair skinned, had light hair, and was around fifty years of age. That is all I remember about his physical appearance. But the characteristic that stands out in my mind is that he couldn't stop crying.

Several years ago, Jeff and I had stopped at a restaurant in Newnan, Georgia, having just visited Mom in the hospital. It was lunchtime, and we had found our kind of place—real home cooking. We had just taken our food off the serving trays when I spotted him.

Directly in my line of vision, in a nearby booth a man was weeping bitterly. I moved my gaze away from him so as not to embarrass him, but after taking a few bites, I glanced his way again. Although tears were pouring down his cheeks, he was obviously trying to rein in his emotions by constantly dabbing his eyes with a tissue. He seemed to be gaining control, so I turned back to my lunch.

A little later I looked up. My heart broke. The poor man was hiding his face with his napkin, but his shoulders were shaking. He was desperately trying to stop crying but could not get a grip on his emotions. Suddenly he grabbed his tray and darted out the door.

Had his girlfriend or wife left him? Had he lost all his money? Had a dear friend just died? I am clueless, but something inside of me tells me that someone he loved was gone. His tears were flowing like rain, his sorrow was so palpable, and it seemed to me that his grief was as deep as the ocean.

I should have done something; I should have said something. Jesus would have, but I did not. If a similar event happens again, I will approach the grieving person and try to ease the pain. I will assure him that I will ask God to fix whatever is wrong. I will offer him a card that all of our church members carry to help others see where the family of Jesus meets and how we care for the burdens of others. I will pat his arm and tell him that he is not alone, that all have problems but our God can fix anything. And if I cannot talk to him in the restaurant, I will follow him outside and offer to help him there.

What did the crying man need more than anything? God! He needed to know that God loved him and that others cared for him. Then we ask: Even if he were to blame for the sorrow that was causing him to weep? Even if he had mistreated the woman who had left him? Even if he were a criminal and just found out he was going to jail? Yes, yes, and yes. The crying man needed hope.

We all need hope, hope that God will fix our sorrows and relationships, hope that God will fix our children and their problems, hope that God will restore us to the family where we once belonged, and hope that God still loves us no matter what we have done.

Does God send broken people into our lives for us to help? I believe He does. Why would He do that? Because we are in God's army, and we work at His recruiting station. Because we are in God's family, and He has told us to gather all those that we can into the circle. Because we are God's ambassadors, proclaiming the love of Jesus. Because we work in God's hospital alongside of the Great Physician, Jesus Christ, who can cure anything and anyone. Because we have been saved and we want others to be saved, too. But most of all, we now know what love really is.

I remember hearing a CD of brother Marshall Keeble's preaching about the trouble going on in Tennessee politics. Keeble said, "The whole world is sick—sin-sick. You know what those people need down there? They need Christ!"

"It's a sad old world," Mom used to say. And that it definitely is. We don't have to turn on the television to know that conflict, abuse, anger, and violence exist in our own hometown. What do we do about it? What would Jesus have us do about it?

He would probably say, "Love one another. Just keep loving one another," or maybe "A new commandment I give to you, that you love one another, even as I have loved you, that you also love one another" (John 13:34–35). He almost certainly would say, "Come to Me, all who are weary and heavy-laden, and I will give you rest. Take My yoke upon you and learn from Me" (Matthew 11:28–29).

We must love others like Jesus continues to love us. We must be on our toes and look for those whom God sends our way. We have opportunities to touch lives and souls everywhere we go: at the ballpark, on an airplane, at the grocery store, in restaurants—everywhere we set foot.

I wish I had said something to the crying man. I will always regret not doing anything that day. I prayed that God would forgive me for not being the light and salt that the crying man needed. Not sharing the hope that is my passion was simply wrong. Whenever I think of the crying man, I ask again for God's mercy on him and on me. There is still hope for both of us.

I have learned that the Pearl Seeker seeks for people to help.

CHAPTER 7

Seek What Is Most Important

Set your mind on the things above, not on the things that are on earth (Colossians 3:2).

WHAT THE WORLD NEEDS NOW

If you were a teenager in the late 1960s, then you are familiar with one of Dionne Warwick's biggest hits: "What the World Needs Now." *What does the world need now?* a young person may ask. Why, that's easy. The world needs love, sweet love. Yes, it does. We all need love, sweet love.

Few of us really enjoy conflict and anger and ridicule. Those are words that describe uproar and chaos in lives, families, and relationships. Usually these words result in broken lives, dysfunctional families, and impaired relationships. Loving words they are not.

Years ago Barbara Walters interviewed Richard Dreyfuss. Ms. Walters asked the film star, "Is there anything that you don't have in your life that you wish you did?" What was his answer? "Yes, I wish I had inner peace." Richard had achieved great success and wealth, even the Academy Award. Many thought Dreyfuss had it all, but he was addicted to drugs and had spent time in rehab. He lacked the one thing that all humans desire: peace in one's soul.

Madalyn Murray O'Hair, the famous atheist, achieved notoriety in successfully removing Bible readings and prayer from public schools in 1963. She founded *American Atheists. Life* magazine referred to her in 1964 as the most hated woman in America.

Mrs. O'Hair wrote in her diary in 1977 that she had failed as a wife, as a parent, and as a politician. And in a half dozen places in her diaries, O'Hair wrote, "Somebody, somewhere, love me" (Sanders, *Search* program).

The world needs love; the world needs inner peace. From the wealthy cinema idol to the ignorant profane atheist and the good people in between, none surprise Jehovah God. He knew our needs all along. That is why He sent Jesus to save us. For some reason, God loves all of us and has provided a way of salvation for all who obey Him. How absolutely marvelous is our God who is love!

> Beloved, let us love one another, for love is from God; and everyone who loves is born of God and knows God. The one who does not love does not know God, for God is love (1 John 4:7–8).

> For God so loved the world, that He gave His only begotten Son, that whoever believes in Him should not perish, but have eternal life (John 3:16 NKJV).

> Jesus answered, "Truly, truly, I say to you, unless one is born of water and the Spirit he cannot enter into the kingdom of God" (John 3:5).

Jesus died on an old rugged cross so we could be born again and have our sins washed away. Oh, what a happy day when we are lowered into the grave of water and then resurrected! It is a day of new beginnings. It is a day of innocence again and having a clean soul. It is a day in which peace and love reign in our hearts again. What once was paradise lost has become paradise found—alive and well.

DO SOMETHING FOR CHRIST

When we become Christians, our sins are forgiven. What is our response to what Jesus has done for us? We want to do something for Him. We are on fire for the Lord, and we cannot wait to tell others the good news of Jesus Christ!

When Albert Schweitzer, the noted theologian, physician, and medical missionary was asked why he devoted himself to the poor in Africa, he said, "I had to do something for Christ!"

Didn't a zealous Paul say that he was compelled to teach the gospel? Indeed he did: "For if I preach the gospel, I have nothing to boast of, for I am under compulsion; for woe is me if I do not preach the gospel" (1 Corinthians 9:16).

What did the Christians do in the first century after having been baptized? Acts 8:4 tells us: "Therefore, those who had been scattered went about preaching the word."

Those "first fruits" of the gospel of the first century were on fire for the Lord. They simply could not stop telling the world about the saving gospel of Jesus. When you find the truth, you have to tell everyone! Isn't it remarkable that the persecution of the church resulted in more and more souls being added to it?

As our family labored for Christ in the mission fields in the Northeast, baptisms were memorable events. The "new creature" came up out of the water, happy and on fire to tell others the good news of Jesus Christ. The feeling was contagious. It convicted us again! It truly was a happy day!

FIRST A FRIEND, THEN A BROTHER

In New England the motto shared from church to church was a motto that works in mission fields anywhere: "First a friend, then a brother." It makes sense to teach our friends, because friends usually listen. But it makes even more sense to make friends of our acquaintances and then share words about God.

Most new Christians we saw were zealous and eager to share the gospel with family and friends. As a result, the gospel spread, the church grew, and oh, the rejoicing that went on!

Please do not think that all personal conversion stories have happy endings. Some new Christians are excommunicated by their families, ostracized forever for leaving the family religion. That is not new, and it can happen anywhere. What courage it takes for the new Christian not to look back, to stay the course!

In *The Begging Place,* I wrote extensively about a wonderful place called Gander Brook Christian Camp in Gray, Maine, operating since the late 1950s. Those who have experienced being a camper, counselor, or just a visitor, share this saying: "There is no place like Gander Brook." In September after the camping sessions have ended, there is a ladies' retreat weekend followed by a men's retreat the next weekend.

The ladies' retreat is among the best! Why? The women come to learn and grow and know God. They are hungry and thirsty for righteousness. This retreat offers deep spiritual teaching, lots of tears and laughter and skits. Throughout the years, the program calls for sisters to tell their love stories. A sister tells how God has helped her. Another tells a story of conversion and finding the truth. A mother shares the story of a wayward son or daughter who returned home. Sometimes we hear of a broken home that God has healed. When I hear these accounts, I sit mesmerized, feeling every emotion of the sister telling it. It is always a highlight of the ladies' retreat.

LOVE STORIES

I will share a few love stories that have been shared with me—some recent and some not so recent. These are not Gander Brook stories but stories of love that you need to hear. As you read, imagine yourself in the shoes of the storyteller.

One afternoon I gathered with some of my sisters in my home state of Texas, enjoying their heartfelt words. We were discussing how we found the gospel, or what made us become a Christian. The women turned to Amy and said, "Tell her, Amy. Tell Becky your story."

As Amy began her narrative, the room grew quiet, and yes, it was a tremendously wonderful and unusual story. Here it is again, just for you.

AMY'S STORY

For quite a while I felt the need to find a church to attend. For years I would drive to a church and not have the strength to even get out of the car. For some reason, I was terrified—not sure of what or why.

One day I received the Heart to Heart pamphlet in the mail from the Magnolia Church of Christ. I enjoyed reading it and decided to attend one Sunday. My husband—neither was he a Christian—told me that if I got the strength to get out of the car and sit through a service, he would go with me one time.

The next Sunday I drove to the church building, scared to death! In the parking lot I talked to God, praying for strength to get out of the car. I got out and managed to walk about twenty feet. Claire, one of the members, saw me and came running over. "You are new here!" she greeted me.

"Yes," I replied.

Claire took my arm in hers and said, "Please sit with me!" That was exactly what I needed! Everyone was so nice and friendly.

The next Sunday I went back, and again I was welcomed at the door. Another couple invited me to sit with them.

A short time later I was baptized. My husband kept his word and came one Sunday, and then another, and then another. He was baptized a few months later.

There are so many touching moments in Amy's story, but what I love most is that when she stepped out of the car, a Christian sister stepped into her life. Then others reached out to her. The brothers and sisters at Magnolia were warm, loving, and open to strangers. They were letting their lights shine.

Oh, my sisters, learn this great lesson from Amy's experience. Christians need to be the warmest, most caring people in the world. We need to care honestly about the stranger who timidly crosses our path and asks what we know about Jesus. Amy prayed, God answered, and Claire acted.

Claire was not doing anything difficult. She was just being like Jesus—reaching out to a lost soul. Why can't we all do that?

While we are sharing love stories, here is one of my favorites. Linda lives in New England, and the story of how she found the Lord is so amazing it is indescribable. Like Amy, Linda was one of those Pearl Seekers who, one day, walked in the door of the church building and met God.

LINDA'S STORY

I'll start when the priest called me before our wedding to ask if I had been baptized. I told him yes. After thinking about it I figured I hadn't since my family never went to church. I was so scared about lying to a priest that I called Kenny, my future husband, and told him.

He said, "Call him and tell him." So I did. All he said was, "Okay, I have to change a phrase in the ceremony." That stuck in my head. I always thought about God even though we hadn't gone to church.

A year or two after we were married, I was still thinking about baptism, so I called the priest at the local Catholic Church and asked him if he would baptize me—but I didn't want to be a Catholic, just a Christian. He told me to come to his office on Monday night at 7:30 to talk. Up I went. He told me all kinds of church history. I loved it, so the next two Monday nights I was knocking on his door. By the third Monday night he told me, "You don't have to come every Monday night!"

He never did baptize me. He told me, "Read your Bible but don't believe everything in it." I thought I'd never understand the Bible. This was in the fall.

Come spring he called. I had kinda lost interest by then. He told me, "I will baptize you Easter Sunday." Well, I was going out of town that weekend.

"I'll call when I get home," I said. I never did. He was moving that fall. On his last Sunday he said to Kenny, "Your wife—I didn't baptize her! Send her up this afternoon." So I went up and got sprinkled.

The following spring I decided I was going to find a church that taught the Bible. I went to a Methodist church because my parents were Methodists. Then I thought I'd go to another. I drove up to two church buildings and read the sign on one, Christian Missionary Alliance. "Hmmm?" I thought. "What does that mean?"

As I sat looking at the sign I noticed another sign on the church next door: "Church of Christ." That sounded better, so I walked in and sat in the back row so I could see who went there. The preacher asked me to move up front. It was a really small group. They were studying the book of John verse by verse. "Boy," I thought, "I can learn if I attend here."

The next week Kenny went to eight o'clock mass. He returned for me and we went to the church of Christ. We were so excited to be learning God's word. The following week after Kenny's mass, we returned to the church of Christ to study John again.

At the Fowler's invitation, we then visited another church that was involved in a study of Catholicism. At the end of the lecture, the floor was opened for questions.

Kenny stood up and asked, "How can we awaken Catholics to what is in the Bible?" One of the elders immediately said, "What hinders you now from coming forth to be baptized?"

Down the aisle Kenny went. But I was the one who wanted to be baptized! So I looked at Lea Fowler and said, "I want to be baptized." Down the aisle I went. The Fowlers were at our house the next night to study the Bible. That was in July of 1977.

Just think! The Fowlers were in Berlin, New Hampshire, studying with others while I was going to the priest, searching. Then the Fowlers moved to Conway and built the building, just as I decided to start looking for the church that was in the Bible. It's like a big tangled web. But it's not tangled. God's got it all figured out.

Amy and Linda are both Christians now in solid congregations.

Let's read about Cammy, a woman from a Christian family who was trying to find her way back home.

CAMMY'S STORY

As a starter, I was raised in the church: ideal home life on a farm, one brother, one sister. My sister attended Oklahoma Christian College and married a preacher.

I ended up pregnant and was married at age sixteen to an ex-con; by age nineteen I had two children. I was in a very abusive marriage, both verbally and physically, but I stayed with that a little more than seven years before getting a divorce. I ended up in another relationship that lasted seven years before I realized that wasn't really what I was looking for.

My church life pretty much ended when I got married. I would find and attend a local church a couple of times if I knew Mom and Dad were coming to visit so I could say that I went there, but I did not attend regularly for more than a few Sundays. It was too hard to get up on Sunday morning after being out all night.

My family was always there for support, as much as I would let them, but most of the time I pretty much shut them out of my life. I obviously felt guilty. I didn't want them to know what I was doing. I knew the truth, but I kept striving to find something other than God to make me happy. Anytime anyone would bring up the subject of church, I would leave the conversation, make some joking comment, or just say, "I don't wanna talk about it." Basically they knew if they were going to keep any kind of relationship with me, they just didn't push religion. My life went on like that for more than thirty years.

My dad passed away in 1998 from cancer. All the family was very close at that time. I took Dad's death very hard. The rest of the family had told him bye and said they would see him in heaven, but for me it was just a little different.

Looking back, all of my family thought surely I would come to my senses after that, but no such luck. Then Kassie and Mark, my daughter and son-in-law, had been studying the Bible with a friend's dad. As a result they were baptized. Of course, they wanted us there for that big occasion, and I'm sure they thought that might get me to thinking.

Oh no, not me. The birth of my first grandchild was a very special moment. Kassie thought maybe that would bring me back. Not so! Because of that precious grandchild I did quit smoking, but that was about as far as it went.

Then a second grandchild was born. Kassie's hope was renewed, but I was not persuaded. She later told me it made her sad that we could never keep the kids on the weekends, because she wanted them to go to church. That really struck home, but still it didn't move me to do what I knew to be right.

One weekend we three kids and Mom were in Elk City to check on Mom's life-long German friend. She had no family in America, and Mom promised she would take care of her until she died. My brother Dub and his wife were staying in the adjoining motel room. They came in to tell us goodnight.

Dub said, "Cammy, I really want you to think about going back to church. You know we're all back in church—me and Jen, Electa and Everett, Mom, Kassie and Mark, and the girls. I'm afraid when we get to heaven, Daddy is going to want to know why we didn't bring you with us. I just don't know what I'm going to say. You know how much he thought of you."

Well, being the youngest daughter, I was pretty much Daddy's little girl, so that hit pretty hard. I promised him that night that I would think about it.

Dub's Bible class had been discussing how wonderful it was going to be in heaven. One of the students asked, "How can heaven be that great if all your good friends and loved ones aren't there?" The teacher responded, "If you don't care enough about them to try to get them to heaven with you, are they really your loved ones?"

That statement really touched Dub's heart, and he decided that he was going to mention me and start praying for me in their small groups on Sunday nights.

They started off by praying that my heart would be softened, that he would know the right words to say and that I would accept them.

Dub started to call me once a week. Each time before he would hang up, he would ask me if I had thought about going back to church. He got several negative responses but didn't give up. Each time he would return to his group, and they would pray for something different that week.

The time finally came when he asked the question again: "Have you thought about coming back to the Lord?" and I actually replied, "I have been thinking about it." Dub was elated. "Great," he said, "I'll be checking back with you."

He reported this victory, thanked God for the progress, and kept praying. The next time he called, I told him that I had not yet returned but that he should not give up on me. He promised he wouldn't! He reported this progress to his group. At that time I had set a goal to worship on a particular Sunday, but something came up and I did not go. I looked up the address of the church and drove by so I would know where it was when I decided to go. I reported my recent activities to Dub in our next conversation. His group began to pray every week that I would find the courage to go.

Finally that Sunday came! I got up, got dressed, and headed to church, thirteen miles away. As soon as I got into the car, I started crying. I cried all the way to town, pausing only long enough to get into the building. I cried all through church. I just couldn't seem to get it together. I kept thinking, "I've got to do something, but I don't really know what." I ended up leaving during the closing song because I didn't want to talk to anyone. I couldn't keep from crying. I drove over to the park and sat quietly trying to figure out what I needed to do. Then it hit me. I needed my brother. He got me into this situation!

I called Kassie and told her I went to church that morning, but now I couldn't quit crying. She told me she was proud of me. We visited awhile on the telephone, but she was an hour away. My brother was on vacation, so I called his cell phone. He was out of range, so I called his home phone and left a message. I told him I'd gone to church, but I didn't do very well. I cried through the whole service and left early to go home. My husband was expecting me, so he had lunch cooked, but he couldn't figure out why I was crying.

Before long, my brother called. He had reached home and had received my message. He and his wife were on their way to my house.

Later, in my living room, Dub began to tell me how proud he was of me. Then he told me that his group had been praying for me for weeks, and he couldn't wait to tell them all about this day! He called one of them to report that he was planning to baptize his little sister!

Time for evening worship was approaching. We called Kassie and Mark. They agreed to come. By the time services started, my sister had picked up my mom who lived an hour-and-a-half away. Also a niece and nephew showed up at the church for this special occasion! Angels in heaven were rejoicing! That was October 5, 2003, a day that I will never forget.

More than a decade has passed, and that time has been the happiest and most blessed period of my life. I hope you will learn from my experience:

1. Never underestimate the power of prayer.
2. Never give up on anyone; they may be waiting for one more nudge.
3. Don't be afraid to confront someone; they may be wondering why you don't talk to them about Christ.

If my story touches one person's life or makes her even think about what she needs to do, it is worth it. I'm just proud of how far I have come and that I'm still an active Christian. It wasn't a "go back for a couple of months" kind of an agreement. It was a life-long commitment.

I figured if God would take me back after all I had done, I had better give him all of me now. I'm so thankful for my brother. How can you thank someone for encouraging the saving of your soul? He says it wasn't him. It was just God using him.

How awesome to meet those who prayed for me all that time! When I introduced myself as Dub's sister, their eyes lit up and they said, "We prayed for you for a long time." Then I told them, "Yes, you did, and I'm so thankful for that. I'm a living, walking, talking answer to your prayers."

But lest we believe that every new Christian immediately finds a perfect niche in the family of God, let's read the story of Tim, written by a dear sister, Marty.

TIM'S STORY

On a cold Sunday morning in early February, just before worship, we met a couple named Tim and Andrea. They responded positively to our greetings, even saying, "We're looking for a church that will baptize us for the forgiveness of sins." But they wanted to study just a little more.

Frank and I set up a study with them and became convinced that they understood exactly who Jesus is and what He had done for them. They wanted to be washed in His blood through baptism for the forgiveness of their sins. So on Sunday morning after worship, the baptistery was made ready. Tim and Andrea put on Christ. Many brethren were there to witness and welcome them into the family.

Family. Interesting word. It implies conversation, fellowship, looking out for one another, growing in our knowledge of one another, and responding to needs in honoring what God has provided for us.

We invited Tim and Andrea to our home for lunch, along with another family, so they would begin to make connections with fellow Christians right away. That was a good starting point. We again invited them for lunch the following Sunday, along with a different family. It was all good.

Others were baptized and placed membership since Tim and Andrea. They too were fully embraced, enjoying all the perks of family. On any given Sunday following worship, small groups are visiting and enjoying each other's company in the foyer and in the auditorium.

But after attending faithfully week after week, Andrea suddenly stopped and Tim sat alone. Oh, once in a while someone walked by, tapped him on the shoulder and said, "Hi, Tim, how you doing?" But the intimate conversations were lacking, especially during our before-and-after visit times on Sundays and Wednesdays. I can only deduce that getting to know Tim is not comfortable for our average members. You see, Tim is blind, totally blind. He cannot intermingle with Christians without some caring brother or sister by his side.

Not only did Andrea stop attending, but she left him. It seems she was looking for a group of people who could look out for him. She didn't want to be his caretaker anymore. She deceived us. Add to this detail the minor point that Tim is battling prostate cancer. He continues to live alone in his mobile home, managing quite well for someone who cannot see. He does not complain. Imagine that! But he does have needs, obvious needs. One of them is fellowship.

The Lord Jesus, after talking with His disciples about the kingdom of heaven (Matthew 25), shares a glimpse of judgment, a time of reckoning. Our God gives us many opportunities to serve Him, to be among those who serve the least in His kingdom. Tim is blind with prostate cancer. He is not asking for help, but waiting. My prayer is that my brethren will recognize Jesus sitting as the "least of these"—their brother Tim.

SEEK THE MOST IMPORTANT THING

I have said it before, and I will say it again: Christians are not perfect, just forgiven. There are many who reach out to the lost and take every opportunity to teach others. There are those who are ready, willing, and able to be involved and do the work of the church. There are those who don't know what to do, so they don't do anything, because it would mean getting out of their comfort zone. And there are those who simply don't want to do anything, period. Instead of standing on the promises of God, they are sitting on the premises of non-involvement.

What happened to the love, sweet love? Has it become unimportant? We can seem to be grateful to the Father for forgiving our sins, and yet show no mercy to the one who needs it the most. When this happens, we who are supposed to be merciful and loving have turned into something we never want to admit: We are unmerciful and unloving.

Remember the parable of the unmerciful slave of Matthew 18 who was forgiven a huge debt by his master only to go and find a fellow slave who owed him a small debt? The forgiven servant then seized and choked his fellow servant and had him thrown into prison! There certainly is no family resemblance here to our Father in heaven, because our Father is full of love and compassionate kindness. How does such a thing happen?

The answer to that is fairly simple. We don't know God. We don't seek His will or His face. We don't know or understand His love because we are immature kids reading all the wrong books and refusing to spend time with God.

We all need to grow up, and that is a lifetime process. We all must stay tuned and focused on God and His Word so we can learn and change. And this means that somehow, sometime, and someway we must stop and make the most important decision we can ever make: to be a Pearl Seeker for the Lord. But sadly, the truth is that not all Christians will choose this.

Trey Morgan, a Texas preacher, says it this way: "Being a believer is easy; being a disciple is hard. Becoming a believer happens in a moment;

becoming a disciple takes a lifetime. Don't be satisfied with just being a believer. Jesus calls you to be a disciple."

I once read a sign on a church building that said:

> We don't change the message.
> The message changes us.

Becoming a Christian changes everything, especially our behavior and lifestyle. It means killing the old girl and putting to death all the sinful ways of the flesh (Romans 6:6). It means getting outside our comfort zone and helping those who need us the most. Remember these words of Jesus:

> Then He will also say to those on His left, "Depart from Me, accursed ones, into the eternal fire which has been prepared for the devil and his angels; for I was hungry, and you gave Me nothing to eat; I was thirsty, and you gave Me nothing to drink; I was a stranger, and you did not invite Me in; naked, and you did not clothe Me; sick, and in prison, and you did not visit Me." Then they themselves also will answer, "Lord, when did we see You hungry, or thirsty, or a stranger, or naked, or sick, or in prison, and did not take care of You?" Then He will answer them, "Truly I say to you, to the extent that you did not do it to one of the least of these, you did not do it to Me." These will go away into eternal punishment, but the righteous into eternal life (Matthew 25:41–46).

When we are helping the least of these, we are helping Jesus too. We forget that. And we forget one more thing: We are the least of these, too, because we need Him desperately. We are also hungry, thirsty, naked, sick, and in prison. What the world needs now is love, sweet love, no not just for one, but for everyone.

Be on your toes, my sisters, God is sending a Pearl Seeker your way. Someone who needs the Lord and is searching for love, forgiveness, and inner peace. You are the key that opens up the very gates of heaven.

Prayer: Lord, help me to seek what is most important.

Song: Lead Me to Some Soul Today

Lead me to some soul today,
O teach me, Lord, just what to say;
Friends of mine are lost in sin,
And cannot find their way.
Few there are who seem to care,
And few there are who pray;
Melt my heart and fill my life,
Give me one soul today.

Digging for Pearls

1. Why is inner peace so important to us?

2. Which "love story" touched you most? Why?

3. How should we treat those who are looking for the truth?

4. True joy is when we seek the Lord, find the Lord, and are saved by the Lord! Read David's inspired words from Psalm 40:16. Circle the words spoken by those who love God's salvation.

   Let all who seek You rejoice and be glad in You; let those who love Your salvation say continually, "The Lord be magnified!" (Psalm 40:16).

Pearl Drop

Father Knows Best

I watch, observe, and wait as I sit in my comfy chair in the most unusual place I have ever been. I watch the people come in the front door, and I watch the people go out the front door. There is one constant here: There is always someone new—filling out paperwork, waiting for his/her name to be called, waiting—just waiting.

I glance to the door on the other side of this large room, the door where radiation therapy patients enter. The door to my left is for chemotherapy patients.

I am here because my husband has cancer. He comes to this oncology center every day, five days a week, and has been doing so for two months. While he goes through the radiation door to the room where he is involved in the battle for his life, I have chosen a soft chair where I can sit and pray and observe everyone in the large reception room. It is a quiet place, because survival is a serious affair. There is not a lot of laughter here, but most people are extremely positive.

Cancer knows no boundaries. It ravages people of all ages, all races, and all walks of life. One day I observed a young mother with her baby girl of about six months. I don't know which one had cancer. Some patients look like the walking dead. Some women have their bald heads concealed by bandannas. One woman that I see every day has a slick head, big earrings, a baseball cap, and one more thing—she is always smiling. She is determined to beat her disease. I cannot help but smile back at her.

I sit here and pray like I have never prayed before. I go to the begging place in my mind and beg God to let my Jeff live. I look around the room and pray for all gathered here, united in one common goal—to survive another day. I pray for healing here. I pray for each of them to look to our heavenly Father and seek His will.

I am most grateful to God for this place. So thankful that there is hope for Jeff and so many others who walk through its doors. I thank God for the doctors and nurses who are so skilled, dedicated, understanding, and proficient, and I am so thankful for all the fabulous technological equipment here.

Soul Mates on the Scream Machine

The radiation door opens and my man walks across the room to me, sometimes he is smiling and sometimes he is not. I know the treatment is very hard on him. I have spent forty-three years with him, and the sight of him always makes me catch my breath. We have been through thick and thin, feast and famine. We watched our two precious children grow up, marry, and become parents. We pray continually for our five precious grandchildren and for their success as children of God. No other success is as important. We have stood together and said goodbye to our parents for the last time on this earth and have been one another's best friend even when we didn't like each other very much. We have survived a financial crisis and learned how to live with the empty nest and a very quiet house.

There is no one in this world who can make me angrier or get me more upset than Jeff Blackmon can, and no one else who can calm me down by simply touching my hand. He always has the uncanny ability to make me laugh. We are complete opposites, but our commitment to God and to each other has produced a surprise to both of us: We have become soul mates. For this we are so very thankful. (We never saw that coming!)

While Jeff was preparing for his radiation treatments, he underwent several CT scans, lots of blood tests, and all the rest. To describe hearing the results of these tests was like riding the Scream Machine at Six Flags. A nurse would call from a doctor's office with good news from a test and off we would soar. Then another nurse would call later and say, “Oh, and by the way, has anyone informed you that Jeff has a spot on his lung? We think you need to see a pulmonologist.” Then we would plummet to the ocean floor. Jeff would have more tests, and again a nurse would telephone and say, “We see more kidney stones. Has anyone told you this?” It seemed that just as we climbed out of one roller coaster car, another horrendous car scooped us up from behind and flung us into the air.

Our eleven-year-old grandson Will was visiting with us when one of these days occurred. Jeff was doing fairly well, and we were experiencing a little peace in our lives. Jeff had gone to work, and Will and I were left to plan our day. I was in the kitchen, and Will was watching TV when the phone rang. It was another nurse, dropping the news: “The CT scan shows something on Jeff’s thyroid. He needs to have another scan so we can determine what it is.”

Sweet Memories in Troubled Times

I hung up the phone and knew that I just could not call Jeff with the news. I had to talk to the Lord first. I went into the living room and turned off the TV. Will looked up at me, and I explained that I had just gotten scary news about Granddaddy. I knelt by the couch and said, “Will, we have to pray right now for Granddaddy. You don’t have to get down on your knees if you don’t want to.”

Will looked at me with his big expressive brown eyes, knelt right beside me and held my hand in his big hands. (He got those big hands from two of his great-grandfathers.) Together we prayed and prayed and begged God to deliver Jeff. Hearing our grandson, who carries our family’s name, pray with such sweet and earnest pleas to our Father in heaven was a moment I will never forget. And I don’t think Will has forgotten it either.

In times of trouble, there are moments of incredible sweetness, and this was one of them. It is certainly true that in the valley of the shadow of death that David wrote about, we, as Christian sheep, experience the best food possible. How could that be? It is a fairly well known fact that shepherds guide their sheep through valleys on purpose, for these valleys are rich and fertile. The sheep need rich food to grow and mature. Our strong Shepherd Jesus knows this. He guides us through these times of horrific and scary crises so that we will partake of His food, trust in His care, and remember His deliverance. And in the middle of this incredible feast and being surrounded by the traumatic chaos of the moment, Jesus stops us and gives us precious and sweet memories. Thank you, sweet Shepherd, for these things.

As much as I begged God for Jeff not to have this horrible disease, I now realize that this was part of God's plan for my husband. Jeff had to travel this path. God knew that this was necessary for Jeff to become the Christian he needs to be. God gives us tests, trials, and sufferings, you know. He says so in Psalm 11:5: "The Lord tests the righteous and the wicked." David, the shepherd king of Israel, affirmed in Psalm 119:71, "It is good for me that I was afflicted, that I may learn Thy statutes."

It is when we are tested that we turn to the Father and beg. When we are in the arms of despair, we are also wrapped up in the sword of the Spirit, the Bible, learning and discovering the truths that have been there for centuries, truths from the Father to His children.

Jeff has now finished his radiation, and so far so good. We are hopeful. We trust in the Lord with all our hearts because we know, having lived this long in the game of life, that the Father knows best. Whatever is ahead of us is all good because we belong to God, and God is good.

How kind the Father is to give us comfort passages to help us in times of great anxiety in our lives!

> The Lord is good, a stronghold in the day of trouble, and He knows those who take refuge in Him (Nahum 1:7).
>
> Nevertheless, the firm foundation of God stands, having this seal, "The Lord knows those who are His" (2 Timothy 2:19).
>
> You are from God, little children, and have overcome them; because greater is He who is in you than he who is in the world (1 John 4:4).
>
> For He Himself has said, "I will never desert you, nor will I ever forsake you" (Hebrews 13:5).

Yes, the Lord knows we are His, and we are so thankful for that. I thank God for Jeff. I am thankful for the years we have had and for what is ahead for us, whatever that may be. I do know one thing: God brought us together forty-four years ago, so we shall just let Him handle every day that comes our way. We trust in Him. He always knows what He is doing. In all these years, He has never let us down.

Like the children of Israel, Jeff and I stand at the Red Sea with dangers all around us. Together we look at one another and listen to God's words through Moses on that momentous occasion: "The Lord will fight for you while you keep silent" (Exodus 14:14).

Oh yes, the Father knows best.

CHAPTER 8

Seek To Be Thankful

Whatever you do in word or deed, do all in the name of the Lord Jesus, giving thanks through Him to God the Father (Colossians 3:17).

Always giving thanks for all things in the name of our Lord Jesus Christ to God, even the Father (Ephesians 5:20).

It does not take much to amuse me or make me happy. Just take me to the grocery store and leave me. Don't ask me why, but I have always loved walking down the aisles, perusing all the products displayed there under one roof. I like to look at all the fruits, and vegetables—fresh, frozen, organic, and unhealthy. Also, I take a gander at the seafood counter and notice the fish with eyes glaring alongside crab claws, shrimp, and lobsters. Then there is the deli with cheeses and cold cuts and aromatic chickens turning on rotisseries. And perhaps best of all is the bakery with the smell of homemade breads, pies, and cakes.

Grocery stores certainly open the doors of our senses! They allow us to smell, touch, hear, see, and sample all kinds of good things!

SHOPPING IN TEXAS

Our grocery store in Texas turns out homemade flour tortillas and tamales daily. We have a sushi bar in the middle of the store with kind young people handing out samples of Japanese rice and fish. (I fought that one for a long time, but finally capitulated when I found out the seafood was cooked.) A man with a tall chef's hat and jacket stands in the middle of the meat section with a grill going and a microphone turned up so that everyone in the store can hear his inspirational comments about the recipe he is putting together before one's very eyes. Our store also has something I have never seen anywhere else: an olive bar. It is the size of a small salad bar, with olives of all kinds, fresh mozzarella, and olive salads in chilled bowls.

Oh, but there is more! There is the lovely flower shop with its fragrant bouquets and gifts. Then there is an electronic department with flat screen TVs, DVDs, and cell phones begging to be purchased. We also have a pharmacy and a host of other departments that display vitamins, dishes, pots and pans, patio furniture, landscaping plants—the list goes on and on. To accommodate local university and college students, this particular store even has a few items of necessary furniture for dorm rooms such as futons, chairs, and rugs.

As I shop and gaze at the magnitude of available merchandise and the freedom to pick and choose whatever I desire, I am always struck by the indescribable blessings God has poured down upon America. I glance around at the many frozen food aisles, the dairy products, and fresh vegetables trucked in from just down the road or flown in from thousands of miles away, and I am simply flabbergasted at the abundance. We are indeed the land of plenty. We are the breadbasket of the world. We are the most blessed people in the world. And isn't it true that most of us take all these things for granted?

I come from a generation that remembers the Cold War, the Berlin Wall, and the fear of the USSR. The nightly news on our televisions constantly ran stories of communist citizens standing in long lines daily to get a loaf of bread or a little lump of meat. We can't imagine what that would be like. We run to the store countless times a week, sometimes for just one item. And how many of us can relate to running to the store for the sole purpose of purchasing a loaf of bread, only to come home with four bags of incidentals—and no bread?

GRANITE COUNTERTOPS, MATCHING APPLIANCES, AND GIMME, GIMME, GIMME!

Now put a peg there and travel with me a little more. My favorite TV programs are home improvement shows. I particularly enjoy two types: a couple searching for a home and a couple remodeling a home. I think deep down I am a frustrated house flipper.

The portrayal of the families in search of a home astonishes me to no end. A cute young couple travels around with a real estate agent. As this couple walks through house after house, the woman says, "I must have real hardwood floors. I refuse to have anything less," or "This kitchen does not have granite countertops and the appliances do not match. This is a total gut job!"

And I say to myself, "Girl, you are so spoiled. Do you know how blessed you are just to have a roof over your head? Many people in our own country live in cardboard boxes and eat from trash cans. And you must have hardwood floors and granite countertops or you won't be happy? How selfish you are, kiddo!"

America is a rich nation and a very spoiled one, too. How many of you reading this were given a car when you were sixteen? How many of you were handed a college education? How many of you have always had clothes on your back and money in your pocket? How many of you have traveled and visited foreign countries? How many of you have beautifully furnished houses to live in and fairly new cars to drive? Do you realize the blessings you had as a young person and the blessings you are receiving now?

Perhaps you have not had everything given to you. Perhaps your parents made you get a job and help in your raising expenses. There is nothing wrong with that. There are many blessings here, too. In fact, it is very smart to teach children the value of money.

GET A JOB

John D. Rockefeller was quite a discerning father; some might even say stingy. Although he had raked in billions, he did not give his children any money when they left home for college. They were on their own. He felt they needed to earn their own way in life.

God has something to say about young people and responsibilities: "It is good for a man that he should bear the yoke in his youth" (Lamentations 3:27).

Why is hard work good for a young man? Having a job teaches him about managing money, being responsible, and working for a living. Furthermore, being employed early in life keeps many a young man out of trouble. Having a job causes young people to consider their future. It also instructs them to comprehend the adages that say, "Money does not grow on trees" and "Everyone has a boss." But most of all, those who begin at an early age to work for a living, begin to look at their life circumspectly—at every angle.

Here's the point. God has blessed us so richly that it is easy to take them and Him for granted even in our older years. Be it necessities or luxuries, we don't usually take time to contemplate what our world would be like without God. Instead, it is natural to want more and more. We just don't stop and think—period!

Here is one of the most challenging passages in the whole Bible: "In everything give thanks; for this is God's will for you in Christ Jesus" (1 Thessalonians 5:18).

What a scripture! Lord, are you serious? You want us to give you thanks for everything? You want us to be happy to be in the throes of heartache and troubled times? Yes, the passage says to give God thanks in all things. Another version says, "Give thanks in all circumstances. It is God's will for us."

How easy it is to be happy and sing God's praises when our lives are going well: Money is in the bank; kids are healthy; the car is running! But just let one of these things go wrong and reality sets in.

A LIFE LESSON

I have learned one thing in this life so far: We don't realize how much we have until we no longer have it. When everything disappears that we loved and thought was necessary for living, it is a heart-stopping moment. God is teaching us to seek Him and let Him help us begin again. That is the lesson all of us should learn, so stop and let the Teacher teach you.

Learn to count your blessings. Are you having a sleepless night or are you lying in bed fretting? As the hymn says, "Count your blessings. Name them one by one. Count your many blessings; see what God has done." Concentrate on the blessings that you do have, not those you don't have. Satan will try his best to keep you focused on the negatives. They are his favorite food.

Someone has said, "The happiest people don't have the best of everything; they just make the best of everything they have." The apostle Paul, who suffered so many beatings, shipwrecks, and insults from indignant Jews, was given a thorn in the flesh by God. He said it best in the epistle of joy:

> Not that I speak from want, for I have learned to be content in whatever circumstances I am. I know how to get along with humble means, and I also know how to live in prosperity; in any and every circumstance I have learned the secret of being filled and going hungry, both of having abundance and suffering need. I can do all things through Him who strengthens me (Philippians 4:11–13).

LEARNING THE SECRET

Paul knew poverty and prosperity, wealth and humble means. However, through these two extremes, he learned the secret of living happily. He learned how to live day to day with God instead of pleasing Satan with his complaints. He was content, no matter what the day presented.

"I can do all things through Him who strengthens me" is about being strong in rich or poor circumstances. However, we cite this scripture and apply it to all the challenges of Christians.

Make sure that your character is free from the love of money, being content with what you have; for He Himself has said, "I will never desert you, nor will I ever forsake you," so that we confidently say, "The Lord is my helper, I will not be afraid. What will man do to me?"

—Hebrews 13:5–6

How can poor people have a love of money? Copy 1 Timothy 6:8 from your Bible. In light of that verse, how can we determine the poverty line? Why does the United States seem to have a serious contentment problem?

____

____

____

____

____

____

____

____

____

____

____

____

____

The lesson of contentment is not an easy one to learn, probably because our carnal minds desire more things. But God has a way of teaching us and maturing us so that we care about Him, not things. It is not always a bad thing to lose what we have or to bring in less salary. We learn to live on less, and we learn that our God will never leave us nor forsake us (Hebrews 13:5).

These lessons are valuable, spiritual, life admonitions that also teach us to have compassion on others who have it much worse than we do. Think about it, my friend. If you had the choice of either having financial difficulties or cancer, which would you choose? Even in poverty or difficult times, the Christian learns one of the most important lessons—that of being content and thankful no matter what the circumstances.

A MAN NAMED DANIEL

Who doesn't love Daniel, that hero of the Old Testament? Surely he never planned on the life God chose for him. He was a prince, a nobleman's son in Israel, with a great future ahead of him.

But the book of Daniel describes his enslavement and that of his Jewish friends by Nebuchadnezzar, king of Babylon, who conquered Jerusalem. Daniel and his friends, all from the tribe of Judah, suddenly were servants in the king's palace. Life, as they had known, no longer existed.

No matter whom he served or where he lived, Daniel set aside time for God every day. Even as an old man, when a group of jealous princes passed a law that would throw him into a lions' den, Daniel didn't alter that schedule. Let's listen to what the Lord says about him:

> Now when Daniel knew that the document was signed, he entered his house (now in his roof chamber he had windows open toward Jerusalem); and he continued kneeling on his knees three times a day, praying and giving thanks before his God, as he had been doing previously (Daniel 6:10).

Every day, three times a day, Daniel stopped whatever he was doing, went into his room and knelt, giving thanks to God. What did Daniel thank God for? Probably for his life—for all things. Did Daniel have a carefree life? Absolutely not, but God blessed him for his love and faithfulness. It seems that everyone knew he prayed and gave thanks to God. Can people say that about you and me?

Do we pause frequently enough and say, "Thank you, Lord"? Do we stop and offer thanks to Him at mealtime? Do we thank Him for providing food, shelter, cars, and jobs for us? Do we thank Him for the money that makes our life much easier? Oh, how the Father has generously looked down upon all of us and given us the necessities of life. And what have we given Him in return? Have we freely and cheerfully given Him anything out of the blessings He has supplied so liberally? "Each one must do just as he has purposed in his heart, not grudgingly or under compulsion, for God loves a cheerful giver" (2 Corinthians 9:7).

What lands in the collection plate on Sundays as it passes in front of us? A few dollars when it ought to be fifty times that?

God wants to hear His creation say, "Thank You." Don't you like to hear words of gratitude? When you have fed hungry tummies, taken care of others, provided home and shelter, and been sensitive to others' needs, don't you, too, want someone to acknowledge your acts of kindness? Sure you do. Sometimes it happens and sometimes it doesn't.

OUR FAVORITE MEMORY VERSE

Think back for a moment. From the time we were little children in Sunday school, we began to learn memory verses. Most likely, we first learned the same one: "For God so loved the world, that He gave His only begotten Son, that whoever believes in Him should not perish, but have eternal life" (John 3:16 NKJV).

There is no other Bible verse that tops this one when it comes to giving. God gave His Son, Jesus, for you, for me, and for the entire world.

In his book, *The Barnabas Factor*, Aubrey Johnson makes a wonderful statement: "Giving is the heart of the gospel and the true essence of living" (99). How true. Jesus is the heart of the matter in life. He laid down His life for us. What would we do, how would we live, and how would we be saved if it were not for His marvelous gift of love? and what will we give in return?

So I ask once more: Have we said, "Thank you, Lord"? Have we thanked Him for His mercy and kindness in forgiving our sins and transgressions? Have we prayed today and asked Him to forgive us of the wrong we have done? Do we talk to the Lord frequently and keep our slate clean?

The world takes God for granted. We must not. Many people never reflect on their behavior or think about what God has given them. They don't question their spirit, whether it is kind or loving. They just say, "Well, that's how I am. You either like me or you don't. I don't really care. It is what it is."

However, when we realize what Jesus has accomplished by dying for us, our hearts are touched, and we thank God for His love. Standing at the cross of Jesus changes lives—our lives! In fact, we cannot say thank You enough!

> *Shout joyfully to the Lord, all the earth.*
> *Serve the Lord with gladness;*
> *Come before Him with joyful singing.*
> *Know that the Lord Himself is God;*
> *It is He who has made us, and not we ourselves;*
> *We are His people and the sheep of His pasture.*
> *Enter His gates with thanksgiving*
> *And His courts with praise.*
> *Give thanks to Him, bless His name.*
> *For the Lord is good;*
> *His lovingkindness is everlasting*
> *And His faithfulness to all generations.*
>
> —Psalm 100

One of the most loved Psalms is Psalm 100. Look at the two lines that teach us about being thankful: "Enter His gates with thanksgiving" and "Give thanks to Him." Here, the child of God is instructed to come before the Lord with a thankful heart and also to give thanks to Him and Him only. He requires us to have a thankful heart and lips. *We are to enter His gates with thanksgiving, not with gimme, gimme, gimme!*

Listen to what Paul wrote to the church at Colossae:

> Let the peace of Christ rule in your hearts, to which indeed you were called in one body; and be thankful. Let the word of Christ richly dwell within you, with all wisdom, teaching and admonishing one another with psalms and hymns and spiritual songs, singing with thankfulness in your hearts to God. Whatever you do in word or deed, do all in the name of the Lord Jesus, giving thanks through Him to God the Father (Colossians 3:15–17).

Here are three verses in a row, stressing how God wants Christians to act. We are to be thankful.

PRAYING BUILDS OUR FAITH!

In 1 Thessalonians 5:17 Paul wrote, "Pray without ceasing." Just three words, but how powerful they truly are.

As we thank God for the blessings He pours down upon our heads daily, we will find ourselves living this verse. We will be praying continually all day long. And that, my sisters, is exactly what the Lord wants us to do.

As we give thanks for this and thanks for that, we see how closely the Lord is working in our lives. We witness the work of His hands in our problems big and small. He calms the troubled waters of our marriages. He helps us raise healthy children and provide food, shelter, and clothing. We reflect on the many occasions in which God has delivered us from the pit of which David wrote, and we are humbled by His love. This is a faith builder, for as we see God's hand mending our lives and providing for us, our love for Him grows.

We observe God's kindness to the whole world, but the world doesn't see it. In Matthew 5:45, Jesus said, "For He causes His sun to rise on the evil and the good, and sends rain on the righteous and the unrighteous."

PRAISE THE SOURCE

The world goes blissfully along, never realizing that the very air they breathe, the very food they eat, and the very life they live are all from the compassionate hands of God. God is in charge of everything in this world. He knows all things. He is the source of all things. He is omnipotent, omniscient, and omnipresent (Psalm 139). He knows those individuals who are murderers, liars, and rapists, and yet He bestows sunlight, fresh air, and rain upon them.

Thank You, Lord, for providing these things for us. Thank You, Lord, for sending Your Son to die for us. Thank You, Lord, for the forgiveness of our sins. Thank You, Lord, for the hope of eternal life with You someday. Thank You, Lord, for the church, our family. Thank You, Lord, for my husband and children and parents. Thank You, Lord, for love itself. Thank You, Lord, for the Bible.

Thank You, Lord, for our homes, cars, food, clothes, toys, lawn mowers, and furniture. Thank You, Lord, for our country and the protection from harm. Thank You, Lord, for our jobs and our health and the ability to work. Personally I am always so grateful to the Lord for soap, hot water, and running water; and for a stove, refrigerator, and washer and dryer; and for indoor plumbing! Thank You, Lord, for what you have done for us today and for what You are going to do tomorrow. Girls, we are rich, rich, rich!

What happened when God's people left Egypt? How did they survive? "They asked, and He brought quail, and satisfied them with the bread of heaven. He opened the rock and water flowed out; it ran in the dry places like a river" (Psalm 105:40–41).

Wasn't it David who was inspired to pen the following experience? "I have been young and now I am old, yet I have not seen the righteous forsaken or his descendants begging bread" (Psalm 37:25).

Thank You, Lord, for Your marvelous kindness in looking out for us and caring about us, Your children. Thank You, O Father, for You.

As simplistic as all of this seems, girls, please realize one thing: God does not have to do a single thing for us! He chooses to love us this much. Why in the world wouldn't we want to tell Him thank You all day long?

MY DAD'S PRAYER

I remember my dad saying often in his prayers, "Lord, thank You for things being as well with us as they are." So I say, "Thank You, Lord, for the status quo." Anyone who has lived long enough knows that everything can change in one second—right?

Later, Dad suffered a massive stroke. Even though he worked very hard to recover from its debilitating effects, Dad limped the rest of his life and used a cane. One day I was at Mom and Dad's home and Dad said these remarkable words to me: "Becky, being able to get up every morning and breathe and walk—these are small victories."

And Dad was right. These *are* victories, aren't they? Aren't we to be thankful to the Lord for them? I especially remember his words now as I roll out of bed and gingerly stagger and hobble around with so many aches and pains due to age. It surely is easy to take good health for granted, that is, until something happens to it. But I am so grateful to be able to walk, especially as I see so many adults using a cane, riding in a wheelchair, or being led about by a sighted guide. Here is one thing I have discovered: There is always someone who has it so much worse than I do!

Frankly, it is tough to grow old; at least, it is for me! The older I become, the more I thank God for life. Moses reminds us: "As for the days of our life, they contain seventy years, or if due to strength, eighty years, yet their pride is but labor and sorrow; for soon it is gone and we fly away" (Psalm 90:10).

CLOSER TO THE LORD

Aging is a privilege. At this stage of the game, the last chapter of Ecclesiastes really puts things into perspective:

Remember also your Creator in the days of your youth, before the evil days come and the years draw near when you will say, "I have no delight in them"; before the sun and the light, the moon and the stars are darkened, and clouds return after the rain; in the day that the watchmen of the house tremble, and mighty men stoop, the grinding ones stand idle because they are few, and those who look through windows grow dim; and the doors on the street are shut as the sound of the grinding mill is low, and one will arise at the sound of the bird, and all the daughters of song will sing softly. Furthermore, men are afraid of a high place and of terrors on the road; the almond tree blossoms, the grasshopper drags himself along, and the caperberry is ineffective. For man goes to his eternal home while mourners go

Take Ecclesiastes 12:1–8 apart. Glean its great truths and see where God describes the deterioration of our bodies: our eyes, our teeth, our frame, and other important body parts and functions. It's really an amazing passage. Explain how the Creator describes the very thing He created—body part by body part!

____

____

____

____

____

____

____

____

____

____

about in the street. Remember Him before the silver cord is broken and the golden bowl is crushed, the pitcher by the well is shattered and the wheel at the cistern is crushed; then the dust will return to the earth as it was, and the spirit will return to God who gave it. "Vanity of vanities," says the Preacher, "all is vanity!" (Ecclesiastes 12:1–8).

After Dad suffered a major stroke, he was moved to the amazing rehabilitation center in Warm Springs, Georgia, which Franklin Delano Roosevelt founded and visited so many times to help his polio stricken body. I will never forget a conversation Dad and I had there. It was a lovely spring day, and we were sitting outside, talking and enjoying the sunshine. The azaleas, dogwoods, and wisteria were in full bloom, and it was simply a breathtaking afternoon.

From his wheelchair that day, Dad brought up a question he had asked me in the hospital after he had suffered a stroke: "Why did God let this happen to me?"

Dad raised the issue again: "Becky, do you remember me asking you why God let this happen to me?" I nodded and he continued, "I know now why this happened. I am closer to the Lord than I have ever been before."

I have contemplated those words many times since that moment in Warm Springs. It was hard for me to imagine that Dad needed to be closer to God, because he was a very strong Christian.

However, I am of the opinion that our Father in heaven is the Master Pilot, taking our lives, guiding our lives, and using the good, the bad, and the ugly events for one purpose—to draw us closer under His wings. We cannot get close enough to the Lord. In Dad's case, a stroke drew him closer.

Is it possible to be thankful for a stroke? Yes, our whole family learned that one. Is it possible to have Alzheimer's and be thankful? Yes, the Lord taught us that one, too. Is it possible to give God thanks in everything—even in cancer and death? Oh, yes. Why should we give thanks in everything? Because God is there, always there in the midst of everything, drawing us closer and closer to Himself. And we give thanks for Him, His presence, and His deliverance. But most of all we give thanks simply because He loves us.

Mom's favorite scripture puts life into perspective for the Christian: "And we know that God causes all things to work together for good to those who love God, to those who are called according to His purpose" (Romans 8:28).

What is God doing in your life, my sister? There may be things that are bringing you to your knees, and that is never bad. It is when we are praying and begging that we find the relationship with the Father that we desire the most. That is what the Pearl Seeker wants the most.

A DREAM OF WHAT HAPPENS IN HEAVEN

I dreamt that I went to heaven and an angel was showing me around. We walked into a large workroom filled with angels. My angel guide stopped in front of the first section and said, "This is the Receiving Section. Here, all petitions to God said in prayer are received."

The room was terribly busy with many angels sorting out petitions written on voluminous papers and scraps from people all over the world.

Then we moved on down a long corridor until we reached the second section. The angel then said to me, "This is the Packaging and Delivery section. Here, the graces and blessings the people asked for are processed and delivered to the living persons who asked for them."

I noticed again how busy it was there. There were many angels working hard at that station, since so many blessings had been requested and were being packaged for delivery to Earth.

Finally, at the farthest end of the long corridor we stopped at the door of a very small station. To my great surprise, only one angel was seated there, doing nothing. "This is the Acknowledgment Section," my angel friend quietly admitted to me. He seemed embarrassed.

"How is it that there is no work going on here?" I asked.

"So sad," the angel sighed. "After people receive the blessings that they asked for, very few send back acknowledgments."

"How does one acknowledge God's blessings?" I asked.

"Simple," the angel answered. Just say, 'Thank You, Lord.'"

"What blessings should they acknowledge?" I asked.

The answer was lengthy: "If you have food in the refrigerator, clothes on your back, a roof over your head, and a place to sleep, you are richer than seventy-five percent of the world. If you have money in the bank, in your wallet, and spare change in a dish, you are among the top eight percent of the world's wealthy. And if you own a computer, you are part of the one percent.

"If you woke up this morning with more health than illness you are more blessed than the many who will not even survive this day. If you have never experienced the fear of battle, the loneliness of imprisonment, the agony of torture, or the pangs of starvation, you are ahead of seven hundred million."

"If you can attend worship without the fear of harassment, arrest, torture, or death, you are envied by, and more blessed than, three billion people in the world. If you can hold your head up and smile, you are not the norm; you're unique to all those in doubt and despair."

—Unknown

And if you can read this message you are more blessed than over two billion people in the world who cannot read at all.

Never give up hope. Our God is working things out, and it is always in His time, not ours. The Father draws us, His children, closer and closer, and there is nothing more wonderful than that. No words can describe the feeling of safety and refuge in God's arms. All we can say over and over is, "Thank You, Lord, thank You."

Prayer: Lord, help me to seek to be thankful.

Song: Count Your Blessings

When upon life's billows you are tempest-tossed,
When you are discouraged, thinking all is lost,
Count your many blessings, name them one by one,
And it will surprise you what the Lord has done.

Chorus:
Count your blessings, name them one by one,
Count your blessings, see what God has done!
Count your blessings, name them one by one,
Count your many blessings, see what God has done.

Are you ever burdened with a load of care?
Does the cross seem heavy you are called to bear?
Count your many blessings, every doubt will fly,
And you will keep singing as the days go by.

When you look at others with their lands and gold,
Think that Christ has promised you His wealth untold;
Count your many blessings—money cannot buy
Your reward in heaven, nor your home on high.

So, amid the conflict whether great or small,
Do not be discouraged, God is over all;
Count your many blessings, angels will attend,
Help and comfort give you to your journey's end.

Digging for Pearls

1. Contrast and compare the grocery stores of your youth and those of today.

2. List some examples of ingratitude you have seen.

3. Is it easy to be content in all circumstances? Explain.

Pearl Drop

The Master Weaver's Plan

My life is but a weaving
Between my God and me;
I cannot choose the colors
He weaveth steadily.

Oft times He weaveth sorrow,
And I in foolish pride
Forget He sees the upper,
And I the underside.

Not 'til the loom is silent
And the shuttles cease to fly,
Will God unroll the canvas,
And reveal the reason why.

The dark threads are as needful,
In the weaver's skillful hand
As the threads of gold and silver,
In the pattern He has planned.

He knows, He loves, He cares;
Nothing this truth can dim.
He gives the very best to those
Who leave the choice to Him.

—Anonymous but
quoted often by
Corrie Ten Boom

CHAPTER 9

Seek
The Hands of Time

Therefore, putting aside all filthiness and all that remains of wickedness, in humility receive the word implanted, which is able to save your souls (James 1:21).

I do not know where yesterday went. I can't even remember all I did yesterday. But it is gone and it will not come back. All I have is the here and now. I have an embroidered pillow that says:

Yesterday is gone,
Tomorrow is a mystery.
Today is a gift.
That's why it is called
the present.

What a marvelous gift God gives us in this treasure we call life. We start out as babes in mothers' arms, then toddlers at the heels, then teenagers at the wheels, then mothers in the cars, and last of all, grannies on the loose! And how did it go by so quickly?

SUNRISE, SUNSET

One day we are rocking our babies and singing lullabies, and then we are sitting in shock as these "babies" parade across the stage to get their high school diplomas. We blink again and hear "Sunrise, Sunset" in the background as one of our precious children walks down the aisle with a lover for life. Then we turn around and experience the blessings of grandchildren—our own child seemingly reincarnated, and our lives are changed forever—again. We look in the mirror and see the faces of our mothers staring back at us. Somehow along the way we became the older generation on Medicare—senior citizens. And we still sit in shock because we do not know how in the world this happened to us. In the midst of all of the chaos and joys of our existence, we all come to this profound conclusion: It does not take long to live a life!

Several years ago I was flying to an "I can't remember" destination, and my seatmate was a delightful gal. We chatted about the brevity of life, and she made a terrific statement that has stayed with me: "You know, by the time we get it together, it is time to say goodbye." Wow, was she right or what?

Time to say goodbye. How can that even be possible? I am reminded of that marvelous passage from Psalm 103:15–16: "As for man, his days are like grass; as a flower of the field, so he flourishes. When the wind has passed over it, it is no more, and its place acknowledges it no longer."

And these scriptures make us stop and ponder:

> Surely every man walks about as a phantom; surely they make an uproar for nothing; he amasses riches and does not know who will gather them (Psalm 39:6).

> We have finished our years like a sigh. As for the days of our life, they contain seventy years, or if due to strength, eighty years, yet their pride is but labor and sorrow; for soon it is gone and we fly away (Psalm 90:9–10).

I remember Mom's pointing out from Psalm 90:10 that there is labor and sorrow in old age. It is very true that our lives are flying by, my friends. Many of us have experienced the deaths of those who were not only our age but even younger. We think we have all the time in the world, but the truth of the matter is simply that life is too short. The obituaries are chock-full of people who thought that death was decades away.

We do not have the time we think we do. We will not pass this way again. Sooner than we think, people will look for us, and our place will be empty. We will not be here. How true that old saying is: "Growing old is a privilege denied to many."

"What do we do with the time we have left?" you ask. Lots! God is not through with us, is He? Of course not. There are people to be visited, dishes to be cooked and carried to the sick, Bible classes to be attended and taught, children to be loved and encouraged, newcomers to be greeted, souls to be led to Christ, and much, much more. Our work for the Lord must not stop just because our hair turns gray and we hobble around. As long as there is breath in our bodies, God is still in charge. He still directs every step we take. It is good to be young; it is good to be old. I repeat, all things are good when you are a Christian! So we must admonish each other to keep on serving the Lord and not fall asleep on the job!

> From the moment God asked Adam in the Garden of Eden, "Where are you?" (Genesis 3:9), the Bible is filled with God's wake-up calls. Like a kind parent who gently, at first, shakes his children in an attempt to wake them, God gently shakes His children in an attempt to wake them from slumber. And if the gentle attempt doesn't work, the wake-up attempt becomes firmer and more serious. God is the Master of wake-up calls . . . We must wake up to our identity as soldiers of Christ, and stop acting as cruise directors on the "Good Ship Lollipop." Christianity is not riding the *Titanic*. We are "in Christ" (Galatians 3:27) where power flows and victory is assured, that is, if we sail on faithfully unto death (Ephesians 3:20–21; Revelation 2:10). (Turner 46, 57).

Let's look at what the Holy Spirit inspired Paul to write to the churches at Rome and Ephesus. As you read these passages, focus on the thoughts of waking up and using time wisely.

> Do this, knowing the time, that it is already the hour for you to awaken from sleep; for now salvation is nearer to us than when we believed. The night is almost gone, and the day is near. Therefore

> let us lay aside the deeds of darkness and put on the armor of light (Romans 13:11–12).

> Therefore be careful how you walk, not as unwise men but as wise, making the most of your time, because the days are evil (Ephesians 5:15–16).

Another version says, "Redeeming the time, because the days are evil." What does it mean to "redeem the time"? Thayer's Greek Lexicon says "to redeem" here means "to buy up, to buy up for one's self, for one's use; to make wise and sacred use of every opportunity of doing good." Is it possible to buy time? No, but the meaning here is to own it personally. If we own time and don't let it slip away, then we can use it for doing all the right things we need to be doing.

> Procrastination is a deadly vice. To put off until tomorrow what needs to be done today is slow suicide. "Lord, make me to know my end, and what is the extent of my days, let me know how transient I am. Behold, Thou hast made my days as handbreadths, and my lifetime as nothing in thy sight. Surely, every man at his best is a mere breath. Surely every man walks about as a phantom" (Psalm 39:4–6). Immaturity says, "You have a life time." Maturity says, "Life is short, and you are living now." God says, "I may come today." We may think we have more time than money. We may have more money. Redeem the time . . . Buy it. Use it. There are jobs today that must be done or prices to pay for them left undone (Fowler 69).

MISSION NOT IMPOSSIBLE!

Jesus was a man on a mission—to seek and save the lost. Oh, how much He had to accomplish in three years! Notice the statement Jesus made to His disciples about the Christian life: "We must work the works of Him who sent Me as long as it is day; night is coming when no one can work" (John 9:4).

God wants us to wake up and act alive as we walk with Him and serve Him, no matter how much time we have left. How important it is for us to shake the cobwebs from our brains and get with the program! We must not sleep on this journey of faith with God the Father, God the Son, and God the Spirit. Walking zombie-like through the motions of worship and Christian living just won't get it.

If the word of God is living and active (Hebrews 4:12), then we must be too! There is so much work to be done, and we are God's vessels. As long as we can breathe, we must do the work set before us. Pray for opportunities to serve the Lord. Meditate on the following scriptures:

> Therefore, if anyone cleanses himself from these things, he will be a vessel for honor, sanctified, useful to the Master, prepared for every good work (2 Timothy 2:21).

> How then will they call on Him in whom they have not believed? How will they believe in Him whom they have not heard? And how will they hear without a preacher? How will they preach unless they are sent? Just as it is written, "How beautiful are the feet of those who bring good news of good things!" (Romans 10:14–15).

I have heard numerous older Christians make this statement: "I want to wear out for the Lord, not rust out!" I thank God for the examples our older brothers and sisters continue to set before the rest of us as they visit, encourage, and remain faithful to the Lord, day in and day out. No, they don't have perfect lives or perfect children. In fact, many of them have experienced great tragedies and yet continue to love and serve God even when their own families do not. Here is a thought-provoking statement about each day spent on this earth:

> This is the beginning of a new day. God has given me this day to use as I will. I can waste it or grow in its light and be of service to others. But what I do with this day is important because I have exchanged a day of my life for it. When tomorrow comes, today will be gone forever. I hope I will not regret the price I paid for it (Anonymous).

EXACTLY AS WRITTEN

There was once a famous playwright who loved traveling from city to city, watching different groups perform his plays. One night he found himself in a small town, watching again a play he had written.

After the play was over, the writer made his way backstage. Upon finally locating the actor, the playwright said, "Young man, I have seen my play performed in many cities across this country. But for the first time tonight, in this auditorium you played this part exactly as I had written it."

What will the Lord say to us at the Judgment, my friends? Will He say to us, "My daughter, you played the part I wrote for you exactly the way I wrote it"? Or will He say to us, "My child, what in the world were you thinking? You didn't have a clue about the part in life I wrote just for you. You never woke up! I do not know you"?

It is a very, very sobering thought. Are you ready, my sister, for the Lord to come today? Are you ready to meet Jesus face to face? How is your faith and where are your works and your love? Someone has wisely said, "Some people live as if they're staying. We need to live as if we're going." As my dear sister Judy in Tennessee, says, "There is more to life than this life." Amen! Preach it, sister!

LEAVE A HERITAGE

A chorus from a hymn in my childhood echoes in my mind:

As the life of a flower,
As a breath or a sigh,
So the years glide away,
And alas, we must die.

How does a funeral affect you? Our tradition of celebrating a life at the time of one's passing is as old as time itself. Something happens at funerals, at least for me it does. Even if I am not too familiar with the one who has passed, there is something about the silence, the songs, the pictures of poignant moments on display, the prayers, and the testimonies given there. Even if this "celebration of life" involves lightness and laughter, there are several questions that always occur to me. The first one is: What will folks say about me when it is my turn to die? (Do you ever think about that?) I fervently hope deep in my heart that there are kind and loving and humorous words said about ol' Beck and not, "Well, she really was a miserable old bat!"

It was my privilege to know and love Loy Mitchell, lifetime preacher and lifetime missionary to Zimbabwe. His funeral was filled with many scriptures and thoughts that were important in his life. As each son, grandson, and brother shared memories with us, one theme was common. He constantly said to all who would listen, "Remember, God loves you." What a heritage to leave our families; what a gift to give others; what a reminder to self of what life is all about. Remember, God loves you. Now my sweet sisters, that's a life lived for God. It's the only way to live, and it's the only way to die.

A funeral is certainly a time of reflection for us all. We think about the brevity of life, and we ponder our progress so far. We analyze our own lives and zero in on what is really important. It's a time of humbleness, honesty, and a real look at the woman in the mirror. And then we ask the most serious questions of all: "If I died today, where would I go? What is my relationship with my Father? Where do I stand with God?" Funerals may be the human's way of saying goodbye. But they surely can bring us up short before the throne of God. And that is exactly where we need to be in the first place. A funeral often puts us on our knees.

James, the brother of Jesus, was inspired by God to write a marvelous book in the Bible. Listen to what God told him to write

Read James 1:22–25 from your Bible. Compare it to the J. B. Phillips Translation:

Don't, I beg you, only hear the message, but put it into practice; otherwise you are merely deluding yourselves. The man who simply hears and does nothing about it is like a man catching the reflection of his own face in a mirror. He sees himself, it is true, but he goes on with whatever he was doing without the slightest recollection of what sort of person he saw in the mirror. But the man who looks into the perfect mirror of God's law, the law of liberty (or freedom), and makes a habit of so doing, is not the man who sees and forgets. He puts that law into practice and he wins true happiness.

—James 1:22–25 J. B. Phillips Translation

____

____

____

____

about that man/woman in the mirror, the hearer and doer. Which one are you?

LIFE'S VANISHING ACT

James again says,

> Come now, you who say, "Today or tomorrow we will go to such and such a city, and spend a year there and engage in business and make a profit." Yet you do not know what your life will be like tomorrow. You are just a vapor that appears for a little while and then vanishes away. Instead, you ought to say, "If the Lord wills, we will live and also do this or that." But as it is, you boast in your arrogance; all such boasting is evil (James 4:13–16).

Mom once said to me, "Becky, do you know what the 'Greek' word is for vapor?"

"No, Mom, what is the 'Greek' word for vapor?" I asked, thinking I was in for a deep theological discussion.

Mom simply said, "The 'Greek' word for vapor is whsst!" (She would zoom her hand through the air to illustrate.)

And, girls, that's how fast our lives fly by: whsst! That vapor called life is here today and gone tomorrow. This passage from James 4 is so true to life! Literally.

We make plans to go to the outlet mall or attend a concert, or we plan on traveling to Europe, but God has other plans for us. It may not be His will that we do any of those things. It may be that our lives will be required of us or that we just stay home! How interesting it is to note that it is even arrogant of us to say that we are going here or going there and God isn't even in the discussion. Instead, we must get in the habit of giving God all the credit by saying, "Lord willing," when it comes to any plans, present or future.

Gayle Forman once said, "We are born in one day. We die in one day. We can change in one day. And we can fall in love in one day. Anything can happen in just one day."

I Counted Dollars

I counted dollars while God counted crosses;
I counted gains while He counted losses.
I counted my wealth by the things gained in store,
But He valued me by the scars I bore.
I counted the honors and sought for ease;
He wept while He counted the hours on my knees.
And I never knew until one day by a grave
How vain are these things that we spend a life to save.

—Anonymous

Redeem the time. "Seize the day [*carpe diem*]," the Roman poet Horace once said. Make the most of every moment of every day. I simply cannot stop at this point without saying this to you, my sisters: Start today and love, love, and love some more! Love one another. Love yourself. Remember, God doesn't make any junk! Love your children. Love your husband. Open your arms and embrace the church and one another. Get out of your comfort zone and love, love, love. Talk about God's love, and then show God's love.

Don't let Satan stop you from talking about God. Don't let the devil keep you from acknowledging God's love in your life and what He has done for you. Don't be timid when it comes to talking about your faith. Satan will do everything he can to keep your mouth shut!

Study 2 Timothy 1:7: "For God has not given us a spirit of timidity, but of power and love and discipline." Satan makes you timid, not God. With Satan you have timidity and fear; with God you have power, love, and discipline. Philippians 4:13 is a powerhouse verse when it comes to encouraging the Christian to live right: "I can do all things through Him who strengthens me."

BE LIGHT, SALT, AND A BLESSING

Be the light and salt Jesus talks about in Matthew 5. Be the love people are supposed to see in every Christian life. Be a blessing wherever you go, so that someday, somewhere, people will say about you and me, "Oh, I am going to miss her. What a wonderful blessing she was to all who knew her!"

Show your love for others now. Don't wait until someone you love is dead to send flowers. Send them today and say, "I love you." Do it now. Let them know how you feel about them. A corpse cannot smell the flowers, feel the love, or hear the words you say at an open grave.

Prayer: Help me, Lord, to seek the hands of time.

Song: I Know the Lord Will Find a Way for Me

I know the Lord will find a way for me.
I know the Lord will find a way for me.
If I walk in heaven's light,
Shun the wrong and do the right,
I know the Lord will find a way for me.

Won't it be grand to hear Him say, "Well done!"
Won't it be grand to hear Him say, "Well done!"
If I walk in heaven's light,
Shun the wrong and do the right,
Won't it be grand to hear Him say, "Well done!"

Digging for Pearls

1. Does your life seem to be flying by? In what manner?
2. What does it mean to "redeem the time"?
3. Is it possible for procrastination to affect our salvation?

Pearl Drop

Women Need Women

I must admit that Mom was incredibly intuitive. She was unusually sensitive to other people and could step back and look at most human situations and perceive quickly what was occurring—negative and positive. She knew how to "cut to the chase" when recognizing a character flaw, and cut quickly. She even had a wonderful knack of observing something and pointing out a hidden fact about you that even you had not even noticed. Enough beating around the bush. I am just demonstrating her wisdom in contrast to my lack of it.

When Jeff and I were young, we moved to a new area and began to attend a congregation that offered quite a few challenges. We had to find our niche—where we fit in. That was not easy.

Tune Out—or Tune In

As we settled in, our family began to grow and we found our comfort zone. Our preacher was a very kind older man, but I felt he was not an "interesting" teacher or preacher. His lessons were cut and dried. I had trouble following him, so I began to tune out his sermons. I found him boring, something I frequently related to my mother.

Then Mom came to visit. When the preacher rose to preach, Mom began to take notes, something she had done as long as I could remember. After worship, we went home to have lunch as usual.

After we had eaten and the kids had been put down for their naps, Mom beckoned me to sit with her on the couch. Together we started discussing the day's worship. She pulled the sermon notes from her purse, and with a strong, compelling voice she taught the morning sermon again to me, point by point.

As she concluded the lesson, she looked directly at me while slowly putting her notes away and said, "That was one of the finest lessons that I have ever heard." I was shocked to hear her say these words, but I was even more shocked to realize that I had missed it—completely missed out on one of the finest lessons a Christian could hear.

How could I have missed such an opportunity to learn and to grow? What was I doing? What was I thinking? I had already prejudged the preacher, the sermon, and even God by tuning myself out so completely. I had not given the preacher a second chance. God had sent us a powerful, life-changing message, and I had closed the door and checked out mentally. As a result, I missed out on the sermon of a lifetime, all because I didn't make the effort to listen carefully and follow the wise teaching of an old preacher. Even if his approach was not particularly easy to follow, I neglected to write down the powerful passages from the mouth of God. That was the least I could have done, but I did not do even that. The power of God's Word, the dynamite of the Scriptures, was laid at my feet, and I turned and walked away in my mind.

As I look back on this incident, I ask myself, "How I could have been so foolish?" I was young and immature, but God had much to teach me that day. I thank God for a mother who loved Him so much that she was unafraid to point out to her daughter the error of her ways, with a lot of love, of course. So much was at stake, and Mom realized it. If I had continued on this blind, deaf, and dumb spiritual journey, I would have missed out on much of the growth, wisdom, and knowledge the Lord was sending in my direction. And unwittingly, I would have led my children to do the same, because children are always watching. I was a young mother who needed to learn a valuable lesson, and Mom unhesitatingly taught it to me.

Listen!

Girls, so many times we think our opinions and perceptions are right when they are not right. We think we have a handle on a situation or even a relationship, but we are as blind as a bat. And that can be very dangerous. Solomon warned us of this in Proverbs 14:12 when he wrote, "There is a way which seems right to a man, but its end is the way of death."

Sometimes we need an older woman to take us under her wing and explain the way more clearly, as Priscilla and Aquila did with Apollos in Acts 18 and as Naomi did with Ruth in the book of Ruth. I am thankful for godly women who will step up to the plate and live the following wisdom:

> Older women likewise are to be reverent in their behavior, not malicious gossips nor enslaved to much wine, teaching what is good, so that they may encourage the young women to love their husbands, to love their children, to be sensible, pure, workers at home, kind, being subject to their own husbands, so that the word of God will not be dishonored (Titus 2:3–5).

Here God inspires Paul to tell Titus to tell Christian women, old and young, how God wants them to live. This is not an easy passage for us. We don't want to read it or hear about it, and we sure don't want the preacher to preach on it. So most preachers don't preach on it. They know if they do, they will be roasted before they get to the parking lot.

We women fight this passage when we should love it. God's plan is for the older women to encourage and help the younger women. (That doesn't take intestinal fortitude; it takes guts.) The tragedy is that most women don't want anybody telling them how to live or how to manage their homes—not even God. Older women do not want to encourage younger women, and younger women do not want to be told how to raise their children and love their husbands. It's that simple. In many congregations the older women and the younger women steer clear of one another. And in the process both lose one of the most precious relationships a woman can have, the love of a Christian sister.

> There is a place for women to learn and to learn quietly. It has always been a principle of God's both in the Old and the New Testament that the men teach the assemblies. But this should not nullify the teaching of God for older women to teach the younger women. There

are as many women to be taught as men, if not more. The older woman has a mind-boggling assignment. She is to be busy helping to instruct the younger Christian women as well as discipling her world.

I've heard young Christian women say, "I don't want the older women teaching me." And I have heard older women say, "I don't want to teach the younger women. I've done my time." However, I haven't heard God say, "How would you ladies like for it to be done?" (Fowler 6).

Help One Another

God wants women to love and to help one another, in spite of their ages. That is His plan. In reality, we know how quickly our lives fly by as just a vapor. It seems like one day we are the young woman with our children at our knees, and the next day we are the older woman, the grandmother, with time to help others. "Yet you do not know what your life will be like tomorrow. You are just a vapor that appears for a little while and then vanishes away" (James 4:14).

I am an older woman now, but I certainly don't feel old. Can anyone relate? I may look like Phyllis Diller on the outside, but inside I am only twenty-four. Anyone still with me on this?

When Mom was dying, my heart was broken. When she passed away, I thought I would die, too. But there were older women in my life, my sisters who loved me enough to wrap their arms around me and say, "Becky, I will be your mama now." Those were the words I wanted and needed to hear. Since then, I have gone to other women who were losing their moms, wrapped my arms around them, and told them I would be their mama, too. This ministry of women goes on.

We women are verbal creatures; therefore, we naturally seek others who will talk to us. We seek friendships and common ground with other women. We do lunch; we text; we send emails back and forth. Why? Because we care about our friends, and we keep the relationship alive with them. Some friends we learn to discard; some friends are good friends; and some friends become our sisters. Just think about the close friendships you have and the kindred spirits, best friends, that you simply could not live without. Remember that old saying: "Laugh and the world laughs with you. Cry and you cry alone"? Well, with women it goes like this: "Laugh and the world laughs with you. Cry and you cry with your girlfriends." Isn't that so true?

My desire is to help women. That is my ministry. I want to help my sisters who are my age and older. My heart goes out to them. But I also want to help my young sisters, from teenagers to those married with children. My heart goes out to them, too. You see, we are all the same age. Why oh why can't we bridge the gap between us and just love, love, love one another? Why do women hold one another at arm's length? Why are we even hateful with each other? My sisters, this should not be.

As a result, the bridge that God desires between sisters breaks and remains in disrepair in many congregations. My precious sisters, God wrote these words in Titus 2 to women, and we cannot walk away and ignore them. God still rules, and the scripture is still there in black and white whether we like it or not. Just think of how much better off the church and families would be if all their women laid their feelings at Jesus' feet, embraced one another, and loved one another.

I remember one of my precious young students named Kristy who grew up in my girls' teenage class and became a wife and mother. She had "graduated" to the ladies' Bible class where we were discussing the gap between older women and younger women from the letter written to Titus. Kristy looked around the table of older women and wisely said, "Always remember. It's not what you say; it's how you say it." How true that is! We must watch our tones with one another and once again, always "speak the truth in love" (Ephesians 4:15). It is always about love, isn't it?

Titus 2:5 says, " . . . that the word of God will not be dishonored." We often miss that part of the passage. It is the bottom line of why God wants older women to help the younger women. This is God's goal in all things, dear sisters. We women are to love one another and help one another so that we do not bring reproach on our Father. We are the image that the world sees when it looks at a Christian woman. We are the image the world sees as it looks at a Christian family. Our supreme desire is to reflect God in our obedience to His precious Word, the Bible.

If the world sees conflict and rivalry between sisters in the church, we have brought dishonor upon the very words of God. Why would a friend be drawn to Jesus if she see us mistreating the very ones we are supposed to love—our sisters? This is serious business.

When it came to her children, Mom took her role as a Christian mother very seriously. She was not afraid to rock her children's boats if necessary. And believe me, she rocked my boat many times. She had a higher goal constantly running through her mind, and that goal was to save not only her household but also those she encountered. Her goal was souls.

I thank God for women like Lea Fowler. I also am forever indebted to the older women who loved me, counseled me, and taught me the way more perfectly. That is what I needed that Sunday in Georgia a long, long time ago when I sat at the feet of a "boring" preacher. I needed help. I needed instruction. I needed Mom's wisdom and her love. And she stepped up to the plate and hit it out of the ballpark. Thanks, Mom, for always being unafraid to say what had to be said so that this girl could grow up right, in the "nurture and admonition of the Lord." It is the only way any life should be lived.

By the way, I never listen to any preacher or teacher now without taking notes. I learned my lesson!

CHAPTER 10

Seek To Be Ready

Whatever your hand finds to do, do it with all your might (Ecclesiastes 9:10).

But sanctify Christ as Lord in your hearts, always being ready to make a defense to everyone who asks you to give an account for the hope that is in you, yet with gentleness and reverence (1 Peter 3:15).

A PARABLE FEATURING WOMEN

I love it when our Lord specifically taught about women, even though the real meaning applies to men, too. Let's read one of my favorites: the parable of the ten virgins.

> Then the kingdom of heaven will be comparable to ten virgins, who took their lamps and went out to meet the bridegroom. Five of them were foolish, and five were prudent. For when the foolish took their lamps, they took no oil with them, but the prudent took oil in flasks along with their lamps. Now while the bridegroom was delaying, they all got drowsy and began to sleep. But at midnight there was a shout, "Behold, the bridegroom! Come out to meet him." Then all those virgins rose and trimmed their lamps. The foolish said to the prudent, "Give us some of your oil, for our lamps are going out." But the prudent answered, "No, there will not be enough for us and you too; go instead to the dealers and buy some for yourselves." And

> while they were going away to make the purchase, the bridegroom came, and those who were ready went in with him to the wedding feast; and the door was shut. Later the other virgins also came, saying, "Lord, lord, open up for us." But he answered, "Truly I say to you, I do not know you." Be on the alert then, for you do not know the day nor the hour (Matthew 25:1–13).

I call this parable a "Judgment Day Parable" because Jesus told this to His disciples to teach them about being prepared for His second coming. Notice that this parable about being watchful and ready is situated at the end of Christ's life and is surrounded by more parables of everyday people waiting for their Master to return. Surely these teachings were heavy on Jesus' mind, for His life on earth was quickly drawing to a close. There was much He wanted to say about being ready and waiting for the wedding feast that occurs in heaven.

KINGDOM OF HEAVEN

Let's take it from the top. What does verse 1 mean: "The kingdom of heaven is like—" ? Jesus is describing those who make up the kingdom (church) as being like bridesmaids, waiting for the bridegroom to come before the wedding and its feast begin.

Our customs are quite different for a wedding. We arrive at the church building and get a good seat before the wedding begins. But if you have seen *Fiddler on the Roof,* you have seen a little of the Jewish custom in Russia at the end of the nineteenth century when the whole village accompanied the bride and groom and their families to the wedding place.

During the time of Jesus, it was customary in Palestine for the groom to go to the bride's house where she was waiting with her bridesmaids. The arrival of the bridegroom was always a surprise; the bride never knew when he was coming. When the groom did arrive, the wedding did not commence until the groom's father said it was time to commence. How remarkably similar this is to Jesus' statement in Matthew 24:36: "But of that day and hour no one knows, not even the angels of heaven, nor the Son, but the Father alone." But one thing was sure. When the groom arrived, the bride and attendants had to be ready.

BE ON THE ALERT!

It isn't difficult to see the parallel of the Jewish bridegroom arriving when no one expected him and the second coming of our Lord. God has not given us a time or date of Jesus' eventful return. Psychics have claimed to know, but God has told us otherwise.

Look at the last verse of this parable: "Be on the alert then, for you do not know the day nor the hour" (Matthew 25:13). What was Jesus telling His listeners? "Watch. Be on the look out. You do not know when I am coming back." That same message is still viable today.

The bridesmaids in the parable were divided in their preparedness for the wedding. Five were wise and five were foolish. Why were the last five called foolish? Because they brought no extra oil for their lamps. They were not prepared for any kind of delay. They assumed the bridegroom would come soon. The five wise bridesmaids brought extra oil, just in case. Just in case what? In case there was trouble or a delay or a mix-up. They were ready for any emergency. Were the five foolish maids bad or evil? No, they just didn't use their brains to think out the whole scenario of possibilities for this wedding event. They were too much in the moment and not enough in their future. It was all about them and not about the bridegroom.

NOBODY ELSE CAN DO IT FOR YOU

Many interpret the oil and the lamps as representing the personal faith and works the virgins had done in their lifetime for the Lord. The wise virgins could not share their faith and works with the foolish virgins because each is responsible for her own salvation. I cannot get you to heaven and you cannot get me to heaven. We can only get there by the preparations we have made while on this earth. After all, isn't heaven a prepared place for a prepared people?

We know that by the time the foolish girls, the ones with little faith and works, rushed to the store and bought oil, the bridegroom came and shut the door. When they called to the groom through the door to gain entrance, he said to them, "Truly I say to you, I do not know you." And there was no more hope for the foolish girls who now (I imagine) were having all kinds of guilt-ridden thoughts such as, "Why oh why didn't I think to prepare myself and get more oil? Why didn't I carry an extra flask of oil? I have a new one at home, just waiting to be used! Why? Why? I have missed everything!"

OBEY TO ENTER

Jesus taught His disciples many lessons that day. His masterful use of parables revealed deep and powerful meanings to be discovered through intense study. I urge you to study them. Our ladies' Bible class studied the parables of Jesus one year. It was a thrilling study, and oh, the discussions that abounded around our tables as we read and reread each one!

The foremost teaching that Jesus wanted to purvey was that we must be ready and equipped for Jesus, our Bridegroom, to return to us. Be prepared! There will be a Judgment Day, and if we have obeyed Jesus' gospel, we will be allowed to enter heaven just in time for a feast that will last an eternity. That is the main thrust of this parable. Let's read these two passages:

> It is appointed for men to die once and after this comes judgment (Hebrews 9:27).
>
> For after all it is only just for God to repay with affliction those who afflict you, and to give relief to you who are afflicted and to us as well when the Lord Jesus will be revealed from heaven with His mighty angels in flaming fire, dealing out retribution to those who do not know God and to those who do not obey the gospel of our Lord Jesus. These will pay the penalty of eternal destruction, away from the presence of the Lord and from the glory of His power (2 Thessalonians 1:6–9).

Judgment Day is coming. Will we be prepared? The above passage is scary. Jesus and His angels will come in flaming fire dealing out punishment on two types of people: those who do not know God and those who have not obeyed Jesus' gospel. They will spend eternity away from the presence of God. That is a great description of hell, isn't it?

NO SLEEPING!

Here is what Burton Coffman has to say about the parable of the ten virgins:

> The parable is practical, the tragic story of the ready and the unready. It applies to all present-day Christians. The kingdom of heaven is the church, aptly set forth in the analogy as a company of precious bridesmaids. The great shock, therefore, is to realize that some, even of these, shall be summarily excluded from association with the bridegroom. The parable is designed to shock men into realization that a host of good, clean, moral, respectable members of the church will be lost. Through sheer negligence, many of the redeemed shall fail to enter in. The foolish virgins are the Lord's own example of saved persons who at last failed to make the port of everlasting life. This warns against idleness and neglect, but it should not discourage. Those foolish virgins did not provide oil, but they could have done so. What was required of them was nothing extraordinary or especially difficult, but it did require concern and attention which they failed to give (*Matthew* 400).

So we have looked at this powerful parable of Jesus. Much is still there to be gleaned and examined. That is the beauty of Jesus' parables. Notice one verse that makes this parable a showstopper, even taking it to the next level: "Now while the bridegroom was delaying, they all got drowsy and began to sleep" (Matthew 25:5). They all grew drowsy. Every single bridesmaid became sleepy and then fell asleep.

Jesus has not returned. Judgment Day has not occurred, and many Christians have "grown drowsy" and fallen asleep. This is the sleep of death. We are still waiting for Christ to come back and take us to heaven with Him. He may not come soon, and as far as we know, the bridegroom is delaying. The possibility of our sleep of death is always before us.

What is the growing "drowsy" part supposed to mean? Aren't you curious? Bible commentator Adam Clark, in his online comments on Matthew 25:4, said this:

> As sleep is frequently used in the sacred writings for death, so drowsiness, which precedes sleep, may be considered as pointing out the decays of the constitution, and the sicknesses which precede death.

In other words, the drowsy part of this parable can refer to the sicknesses which typically come before death. Just think about it: heart attacks and strokes happen before someone finally passes on. Long illnesses such as cancer and Parkinson's disease rob one of mobility and ability. And what about dementia and Alzheimer's that cause a person gradually to slip into oblivion, not knowing family or places or things before death finally arrives?

Yes, a human can be very sick, can grow drowsy before the final sleep of death occurs. Life is short; days are flying by too fast. We don't know what is ahead of us, but childishly we think that we still have all the time in the world, when in reality, we may have only a day, a week, or a year. Who knows when death will come or when Jesus will return? Both will be a surprise.

WILL GOD TAKE AWAY YOUR EXCUSE?

"I would love to go to a Bible lectureship and learn more about God. I will do that one of these days," someone says. Or maybe it's "I want very much to attend the weekly ladies' Bible class. I would love to be a part of the prayer circle. Someday I'll do that," or "One of these days I am going to go to a ladies' retreat or a ladies' day but not right now." Oh, there is time for shopping, but no time for the Lord.

We think we have all the time in the world, but that "time" never seems to come. Our plans to grow closer to God and to become a more spiritual woman may never happen because the "drowsy part" knocks on our door, and we are totally unprepared. We don't realize that we may "grow drowsy" with some kind of sickness and be unable to live life as we know it. The time we thought we had might disappear, never to return.

We may have a stroke and be unable to walk or talk; we may have a bout with cancer and become bedridden; our mind may begin to slip and we lose the memory of God's Word; and with that loss of memory, gone forever are all the things we meant to do for God and with God. Instead, our minds are flooded with all the "shouldas," "wouldas" and "couldas." Then we no longer have the excuse of "I'll do it someday."

Gone is the spiritual bucket list. Gone are the opportunities to travel to lectureships and learn and grow. Gone are the plans to attend a Tuesday morning ladies' Bible class and pray with the sisters. Gone is the mind that once knew all the books of the Bible backwards and forwards. Never to materialize are the plans to be like Mary who sat at the Lord's feet and studied His Word. These things are gone because we have selfishly chosen shopping, sports, and events over God. Gone are all the opportunities that were extended to us three times every week, year in and year out, to really know who the Father is and His plans for us. All gone.

If it doesn't take long to live a life, then it surely doesn't take long to die. People will look for us, but we will no longer be there because that flower called our life is gone. Let's read David's lines one more time.

> As for man, his days are like grass;
> As a flower of the field, so he flourishes.
> When the wind has passed over it, it is no more,
> And its place acknowledges it no longer (Psalm 103:15–16).

WAKE UP!

Listen, my sisters. Please hear me, my sisters. Wake up, my sisters! Don't go to sleep, my sisters. Let's live! Let's live and do and learn and grow while we still can, while we have a brain and can still remember. Let's go to that Bible lectureship and go to that ladies' Bible class and take that mission trip while we can still get around! Let's work on our prayer life and go and visit the sick. We don't know what tomorrow will bring. We may not even have tomorrow. Death may come tonight. Our souls may be required of us this very evening. Then will the Father call us a fool like He did the rich man who was unprepared for eternity in Luke 12?

> But God said to him, "You fool! This very night your soul is required of you; and now who will own what you have prepared?" So is the man who stores up treasure for himself, and is not rich toward God (Luke 12:20–21).

Will the Bridegroom Jesus say through a closed door, "I do not know you"? Bronnie Ware is a nurse and an author. In one of her blogs, she spoke of some of the regrets of terminal patients. Listen to her words.

REGRETS OF THE DYING

For many years I worked in palliative care. My patients were those who had gone home to die. I was with them for the last three to twelve weeks of their lives. People grow a lot when they are faced with their own mortality. When questioned about any regrets they had or anything they would do differently, common themes surfaced again and again. Here are the most common five:

1. *"I wish I'd had the courage to live a life true to myself, not the life others expected of me."* This was the most common regret of all. When people realize that their life is almost over and look back clearly on it, it is easy to see how many dreams have gone unfulfilled.
2. *"I wish I hadn't worked so hard."* (This came from every male patient that I nursed.) They missed their children's youth and their partner's companionship. Women also spoke of this regret. All of the men I nursed deeply regretted spending so much of their lives on the treadmill of a work existence.
3. *"I wish I'd had the courage to express my feelings."* Many people suppressed their feelings in order to keep peace with others. As a result, they settled for a mediocre existence and never became who they were truly capable of becoming.
4. *"I wish I had stayed in touch with my friends."* Often they would not truly realize the full benefits of old friends until their dying weeks and it was not always possible to track them down. Many had become so caught up in their own lives that they had let golden friendships slip by over the years. There were many deep regrets about not giving friendships the time and effort that they deserved. Everyone misses their friends when they are dying.

5. *"I wish that I had let myself be happier."* This is a surprisingly common one. Many did not realize until the end that happiness is a choice. They had stayed stuck in old patterns and habits. Fear of change had them pretending to others and to themselves that they were content. When deep within, they longed to laugh properly and have silliness in their lives again.

When you are on your deathbed, what others think of you is a long way from your mind. How wonderful to be able to let go and smile again, long before you are dying.

Her words really make us think, don't they? Yes, our lives are short, but shouldn't the end here on earth be as peaceful as possible? We fret too much about our final hours, when all the time, God has said to us, "Precious in the sight of the Lord is the death of His godly ones" (Psalm 116:15).

If the Lord says our death is precious in His sight, then we will just have to let go and trust Him on that. Whenever our death comes and whatever the circumstances, I believe the Lord will make it sweet. How wonderful it will be to close our eyes and hear the Father say, "Let go, child, I'll take it from here."

Prayer: Lord, help me seek to be ready.

Song: Hold to God's Unchanging Hand

Time is filled with swift transition,
Naught of earth unmoved can stand,
Build your hopes on things eternal,
Hold to God's unchanging hand.

Chorus:
Hold to God's unchanging hand,
Hold to God's unchanging hand;
Build your hopes on things eternal,
Hold to God's unchanging hand.

Trust in Him who will not leave you,
Whatsoever years may bring,
If by earthly friends forsaken
Still more closely to Him cling.

Covet not this world's vain riches
That so rapidly decay,
Seek to gain the heav'nly treasures,
They will never pass away.

When your journey is completed,
If to God you have been true,
Fair and bright the home in glory
Your enraptured soul will view.

Digging for Pearls

1. How does a funeral affect you?

2. How can I seize the day for God?

3. Why is it so important to show our love for others now?

Pearl Drop

Real Life

Have you ever stopped to think about the unusual people and events that God has sent your way? I have always considered the saying, "Truth is stranger than fiction," to be right on target! When contemplating the various characters—some weirdoes; some unbelievable—and wondrous facts of my life, I realize that if I actually wrote my life story, many would not believe it! Even if Hollywood were to make a movie of ol' Beck's life, the producers probably would categorize it as science fiction.

Reflect on the people you have known and the many encounters that have had profound effects on your life. Consider God's role in these. Also realize that Satan has introduced you to people who exerted the wrong kinds of influence. While you are doing all the pondering, read the following true events and see if they have a common thread. I think they do.

The Child

Lily is the grandchild of Patty, my sister in Christ. Patty's son and daughter-in-law live in a western state and have decided to raise her without God. When Lily was eight years old, she was visiting Patty. At breakfast Patty led a prayer, as she did before every meal. She asked her guests to bow their heads and began with, "Dear God . . ." Immediately after the prayer, Lily blurted out, "Who is God?"

The Soldier

If you travel by air, you are certainly familiar with the TSA, the organization that searches you and your belongings before you board an airplane. They are a threat to terrorists who want to hurt travelers. I am most appreciative of their presence and job.

I make it a point to express gratitude to them, because they encounter many who insult them—"ugly Americans," as they are often called. My favorite expressions to TSA agents are "God is good," and "God is in charge." Most agents nod their head and smile. Some even add, "All the time!" I want to be a blessing in their day, not a curse.

At the Killeen airport in Texas, always filled with soldiers and other military personnel, I recently passed through the check point and greeted a TSA agent with my usual thanks and blessing. A young soldier said, "Ma'am?"

"Yes?" I replied.

"I just wanted to tell you how much I appreciate your faith in God and your willingness to tell others about Him."

That was the start of a most interesting conversation about the Lord and His goodness. The young man told me how much he loved Jesus. After several minutes, as he turned to go, I said, "Be sure to read your Bible. God has all the answers in there."

He quickly replied, "Oh, no, ma'am. I don't read the Bible." And he walked away.

I stood there stunned. How in the world can you love Jesus but not read the Bible? How can you have a relationship with the Son of God if you don't know who He is? The answer is, you cannot love Jesus or know Jesus without the words of God. It doesn't compute. One and one does not make three. Remember Jesus' words to those trying to test Him? "You are mistaken, not understanding the Scriptures, or the power of God" (Matthew 22:29).

Without Knowledge

God inspired Paul to write specifically about this very same problem. Those who had studied God's law over the years crucified Christ. They should have known that He was the true Son of God, but they didn't. They said they loved God but they did not know Him. They simply were not in the Word enough. They had a zeal for God but were without knowledge, as was the young soldier in Killeen.

> For I testify about them that they have a zeal for God, but not in accordance with knowledge. For not knowing about God's righteousness and seeking to establish their own, they did not subject themselves to the righteousness of God (Romans 10:2–3).

God does not want anyone to be lost: "The Lord is not slow about His promise, as some count slowness, but is patient toward you, not wishing for any to perish but for all to come to repentance" (2 Peter 3:9). Listen to the comparable verse, 1 Timothy 2:3–4: "This is good and acceptable in the sight of God our Savior, who desires all men to be saved and to come to the knowledge of the truth." The God of second chances wants us to wake up, get into His Word, and find the truth. How important it is for us to have a zeal for God that is backed up by divine scriptures! How important it is to have knowledge of God's precious Word. When we study and ask questions, God fills in the blanks and grounds our faith to the point that we become "steadfast, immovable, always abounding in the work of the Lord, knowing that your toil is not in vain in the Lord" (1 Corinthians 15:58).

The Old Couple

I will always be able to see them sitting there. They sometimes sat side by side on the couch. Sometimes he sat in his chair and she sat in hers, and sometimes they were propped up in bed together. But whatever the position, my parents read their Bibles together, out loud and side by side, every day as they journeyed through life. Reading God's precious Word was never an option for them; it was a must. Skipping a daily reading never crossed their minds. Learning and growing in the admonition of the Lord was their highest calling—a lifetime task. Together they were His. Together they lived for Him and served Him. Together they walked into eternity with Him. My parents did everything together. They loved, laughed, fought, argued, and then laughed and loved all over again. Their life was just like that.

The picture of them reading their Bibles together will forever be stamped in my memory, because it was the thing they loved to do the most. They did not simply read a passage and put their Bibles away. There were always questions: "Why did God do that, do you suppose?" "What happened to her, do you think?" "Where is that scripture that is just like this one?" These are just a few. Usually a discussion occurred after their Bible reading, as their time for God was not over. It was a time for learning, growing, and loving God more. And what an impression it made on me!

How did Mom and Dad stay so strong all those years? I know that whenever I needed strength and help and guidance, I ran home. My parents were always there for me. But where did they go when they needed help? Their parents were not there for them. What did Mom and Dad do?

And I see them again in my mind, sitting together in their den, talking to one another and reading the Bible with one another. God was their strength from the very beginning of their lives with each other. As they became Christians together, Mom and Dad looked to God at every bend of the road, every crisis, every joy, every problem, every undertaking—just everything.

God was their mother and their father. Mom and Dad experienced so many difficulties: job changes, job losses, a daughter with a brain tumor, church woes, and health crises. But God delivered them. They most certainly lived Psalm 34:19: "Many are the afflictions of the righteous, but the Lord delivers him out of them all."

I understand that now. I still long to run home to Mom and Dad and throw everything at their feet, but they are not there anymore. However, I know what they would say. "What do you think the Lord wants you to do?" "Let's give this to the Lord and let him handle it." "You are never alone, so let's stop and pray." They knew the power of prayer. They had learned long ago to trust in the Lord with all their hearts. For them it was the only way to live.

You see, my parents were Pearl Seekers. They were curious, eager to learn, ready to do whatever the Lord said to do, seeking His face and

His will. Their eagerness was contagious to me and to all who knew them. You just cannot be around positive, loving, and spiritual people without their character and habits rubbing off on you. God knows that, so He puts wonderful Christians in our lives to help us, guide us, and encourage us along our journey. Many times these people are our parents. Once again, we realize that God knows just what we need. We are never alone.

These three stories reveal how we men and women approach God and what decisions we make concerning Him in our lives. We question who He is. We may even love Him, but we don't have a clue what the Bible says about Him. And we may choose to read His Book all the days of our lives.

CHAPTER 11

Seek To Know God Is Real

But the Lord is the true God; He is the living God and the everlasting King (Jeremiah 10:10).

Apart from motherhood, schoolteachers have the most difficult job. They are never paid enough for the work they must do, the material they have to cover, the students they must deal with, and the parents who know no boundaries. If you are not a teacher, you just don't understand the stress or the burdens.

When I taught school, a certain scene repeated itself several times. (Keep in mind that the students involved in this scene were eighth graders, about fourteen years of age.) The scene went something like this: "Mrs. Blackmon, I have a question. Can you tell me how much work I have to do to just pass? I just want to make a C in this class. That's all I care about."

Standing before me was the epitome of laziness, an evader of both class and homework assignments. He didn't want to read, and he surely didn't want to study for an exam. A book report was agony to him and a project or term paper was out of the question. "Don't make me do any work" was his motto, and "Don't make me learn" was his creed. That was his philosophy and would be, most likely, for the rest of his life. My class was just the beginning of his lifetime pattern called "just getting by," and it irritated the stew out of me. That kind of attitude, blatant and in my face, infuriated the teacher in me that wanted nothing more than to teach and to help. A teacher and friend once told me, "You are in your classroom doing everything you can to teach your subject, and the students are in your classroom doing everything they can to keep you from teaching." I cannot tell you how true that was.

It takes quite a lot of courage or gall—or maybe stupidity!—to ask a teacher these questions. Naturally, all kinds of snappy and smart retorts went through my head, but usually my reply went something like this: "Really? Please have a seat."

ARISTOCRACY OR MEDIOCRITY?

Even as I write this, it amazes me that any human would choose to be content with mediocrity. Would we ever do such a thing? "Oh, no! Only immature kids think this way." Are you sure about that?

Would we ever approach our boss with these questions: "What can I do just to get by on this job?" or "What is the minimum work I can do for you and still draw my salary?"

"Of course not!" is our instant reply. We know the consequences of such a question: a pink slip and a door marked "EXIT"!

A manager of a business once said, "Most folks work just hard enough to keep from being fired, and the company pays them just enough to keep them from quitting." Sadly, that is often the case.

Have we stopped and considered how we treat God, our loving Father, the one in charge of our lives and everything around us—the real Boss? Do we approach the throne of God and ask, "Lord, how much do I have to do to be saved? Lord, what is the least amount of work I have to do to make it to heaven? Lord, how faithful do my family and I have to be? Lord, how much do I have to do just to get by? Lord, how much of me do You require?"

We don't want to be a daily Bible reader; we don't want to put forth the effort to be more faithful; and we surely don't want to attend the gospel meeting. We want to sit back and let the teacher or preacher do all the work. "Please don't make me study, God; don't make me read anything; don't make me go to church," we say in our minds.

We don't want to grow; we don't want to help the teacher; we don't want to do anything. We just don't want to "do the work" to know God. Frankly, we don't want to serve Him. We don't want—. Aren't we acting just like those arrogant, lazy fourteen-year-old children with no sense in their bones about being responsible and right and pleasing in God's sight?

As children of the King, we must never be satisfied with being mediocre. We are royalty with responsibilities.

HOW MUCH DOES HE WANT?

I once heard Dr. Jim Gardner, a Bible professor at Freed-Hardeman University, make a very profound statement about God: It was his practice to ask his students, "What does God want from you?"

The students replied with answers like these: "God wants our talents," "God wants our love," and "God wants our time."

After a discussion, Dr. Gardner would inform his class in words similar to these: "What does God want from you? He wants *all* of you." How absolutely right! God wants every talent, every thought, every work, every single bit of us. He wants total commitment. And why shouldn't He? We have surrendered all; we have put our hand to the plow and not looked back; we have crossed the line; and we are choosing the Pearl over anything in life. Remember, a halfhearted Christian cannot serve a wholehearted Savior.

C. S. Lewis once penned some profound thoughts. Keep in mind that he is imagining what God would say:

> Give me all. I don't want so much of your time, and so much of your money and so much of your work. I want you! I have not come to torment your natural self but to kill it. No half measures are any good. I don't want to cut off a branch here and a branch there. I want to have the whole tree down. Hand over the whole natural self, all the desires which you think innocent as well as the ones you think wicked, the whole outfit. I will give you a new self instead. In fact, I will give you Myself. My own will shall become yours.

SEARCH THE SCRIPTURES

Girls, we must ask ourselves how we really feel about God! Are we like the youngster who does not know who God is, or the soldier who never reads the Bible, or the student who does not desire to work? Or are we like the old couple dedicated to the Lord?

Do we honor Him and stand in awe of Him? Do we want to sit at His feet and learn? Do we want to please Him, or do we foolishly believe that our parents can somehow pave our way to heaven? Remember, we cannot entrust our spiritual growth and salvation to someone else! It is impossible for anyone to get us to heaven. That is our job. It's true, too many Christians are convinced, but not converted.

Once I traveled with several Christians to Sunday morning worship in another state. We sang and prayed together. Then the preacher rose to deliver his message. I had my Bible in my lap, ready to go, wanting to follow along in the Scriptures, but there was just one problem: As he walked to the podium, someone dimmed the lights so much that I could not read.

We were like an audience in a theater—in the dark. The stage was the focus. Talk about a perfect opportunity to sleep; this was certainly it! The message that I got that day was just relax and let the preacher do all the work. It doesn't matter if he preaches the truth or not, you just go with the flow.

But I can't go with the flow. I am responsible for the most important thing I know—my own soul. When Jesus comes at Judgment Day, I will have to answer for my decisions about Him and how I have conducted my life. I will answer for the words I have uttered in my daily walk. I will also be responsible for what I, as God's teacher, have taught others.

> But I tell you that every careless word that people speak, they shall give an accounting for it in the day of judgment. For by your words you will be justified, and by your words you will be condemned (Matthew 12:36–37).

A STRICTER JUDGMENT

There will come a day when teachers and preachers will have to give an account for what they instructed others to think, believe, and do. The Bible says, "Let not many of you become teachers, my brethren, knowing that as such we will incur a stricter judgment" (James 3:1). Elders and deacons will have to answer for how they led the flock and the example they set before them. God urged elders:

> Shepherd the flock of God among you, exercising oversight not under compulsion, but voluntarily, according to the will of God; and not for sordid gain, but with eagerness; nor yet as lording it over those allotted to your charge, but proving to be examples to the flock (1 Peter 5:2–3).

To whom much is given, much is required (Luke 12:48). You and I will stand before the Judgment Seat of God, and we will answer for our lives, the choices we made, and how we used our God-given talents. All secrets will be revealed as we stand before the throne of the Father. Nothing will be hidden. At the end of the day, God still rules and God still wins, no matter what. I have to face that. And so do you.

DEFENSE: IT'S UP TO ME

With every temptation that Satan thrust at Jesus in Matthew 4, our Savior replied, "It is written," every single time. The Word that was breathed from the very lips of our Father, the Word that was written down by holy men inspired by God, and the Word that became flesh and dwelt among us—this Word is alive and well, working in our hearts and saving men's souls today. How well do we know Him and how well do we know His Word? Are we able to defend our faith by saying, "It is written"?

We have already mentioned Colossians 3:16, but here it is again, and what a powerhouse passage it is!

> Let the word of Christ richly dwell within you, with all wisdom teaching and admonishing one another with psalms and hymns and spiritual songs, singing with thankfulness in your hearts to God (Colossians 3:16).

Isn't it intriguing that this passage says to let the Word richly dwell within you; not dwell in someone else, but you! I am responsible for my own soul. I am responsible for how much I personally study the Bible. No one can do that for me. I am the only person who decides how spiritual I really want to be.

> The expression, "word of Christ," can mean either the word from Christ or the word about Christ. It may even embrace both senses. Christians are to let the "word" take up residence within them by study, reflection, the example of others, and personal action (Jackson 423).

What is the opposite of the word *richly*? It is "poorly." Consider the following contrasts:

1. I can be a daily Bible reader, following along in my Bible with teachers and preachers as they speak God's message, and the end result will be that the Word of Christ richly dwells within me. I can quote important passages in the Word to guide me through hard times and comfort me in tough times. What is the result? My soul is healthy; my faith is fortified, and I am maturing as the Word changes my life. My relationship with God is strong because I know He is my Rock.

2. I can sit back, relax, and let everyone else do the work while I do nothing to exert my brain toward spiritual growth, and the end result will be that the Word of Christ poorly dwells in me and in my life. I can't quote much scripture because I am not listening, and my soul is sick. There is nothing which I can rely on or cling to.

I am the only one responsible for the fate and state of my soul, rich or poor.

SEEK; GOD WILL LET YOU FIND HIM

God has seen to it that His powerful and mighty Word reveals instances of people who sought Him, served Him, and rejected Him. God is always trying to tell us something in the Bible. Let us look at a few seekers:

1. *Rich young ruler* (Mark 10:17–22). The price of serving God was too high for him. He refused to give up his riches and become Jesus' disciple. This seeker said no to God.

2. *Solomon* (Ecclesiastes 1:17). The man God richly blessed with wisdom and riches set his mind to know wisdom, madness, and folly, and his heart was turned away from God. This seeker lost his way.

3. *Asa, king of Judah* (2 Chronicles 15:2). At the beginning of his reign, He was told, "The Lord is with you when you are with Him. And if you seek Him, He will let you find Him; but if you forsake Him, He will forsake you." As a result, the tribes of Judah, Benjamin, Ephraim, Manasseh, and Simeon made a covenant with God. Look at the Pearl Seekers here, five tribes of God's people. See how God blessed them for looking for Him, loving Him, and living for Him:

   > So they assembled at Jerusalem in the third month of the fifteenth year of Asa's reign. They sacrificed to the Lord that day seven hundred oxen and seven thousand sheep from the spoil they had brought. They entered into the covenant to seek the Lord God of their fathers with all their heart and soul; and whoever would not seek the Lord God of Israel should be put to death, whether small or great, man or woman. Moreover, they made an oath to the Lord with a loud voice, with shouting, with trumpets and with horns. All Judah rejoiced concerning the oath, for they had sworn with their whole heart and had sought Him earnestly, and He let them find Him. So the Lord gave them rest on every side (2 Chronicles 15:10–15).

   The flip side of this success and prosperity was abandonment by God. That also happened to the once-good King Asa (2 Chronicles 16:7–12). Seeking, serving, and rejecting—all found in one character.

4. *Nicodemus* (John 3:1–11). He came by night, feeling compelled to ask Jesus pressing questions. You can feel the urgency as he queries, "How can these things be?" Later, in John 7:50–51, we see a changed Nicodemus, questioning his Jewish colleagues. The last time we see Nicodemus (John 19:39), he is no longer afraid of the Pharisees or

the Sanhedrin. He boldly accompanies Joseph of Arimathea with heavy and expensive perfumes in order to give the Son of heaven the burial of a prince. Nicodemus was a Pearl Seeker.

5. *Timothy*. This preacher was a fine, outstanding young man. Raised by two very spiritual women, Lois and Eunice, he preached the Word, accompanied Paul on missionary journeys, and loved the Lord. Paul admonished him to continue seeking:

   > You, however, continue in the things you have learned and become convinced of, knowing from whom you have learned them, and that from childhood you have known the sacred writings which are able to give you the wisdom that leads to salvation through faith which is in Christ Jesus (2 Timothy 3:14–15).

   Lois and Eunice were dedicated and committed Pearl Seekers who raised their son and grandson Timothy to be a Pearl Seeker too, one who would continue to go, teach, and save others. Is there anything better than that?

What are we doing for the Lord, my sisters? Are we talking to our children and grandchildren about Him? Are we raising them to seek Him and His marvelous face? What heritage are we leaving them?

Are we looking for opportunities to tell others about the marvelous saving grace of our God? Are we studying, growing, and learning more about our God every day? Are we a blessing to others? Are we seeking, expecting that God will let us find Him?

GROW UP!

Someone once said, "If everyone could just get a glimpse of either heaven or hell, the church buildings would be full." Oh, how true that is! How would your life change? What would you do differently?

Paul gave us a personal glimpse of his growth:

> When I was a child, I used to speak like a child, think like a child, reason like a child; when I became a man, I did away with childish things (1 Corinthians 13:11).

It is time for us to grow up, my sweet sisters. It's time to stop being a child who wants the easy way out. It is time to get serious and to put away all the lazy and childish things that prevent us from being the daughter of the King we can be and ought to be.

How merciful, kind, and loving the Father has been with us, waiting for us to mature and say no to Satan and to expel for good that fourteen-year-old that lives inside our brain.

STATUS QUO IS A NO

We have a higher calling than just being concerned with the status quo. Marshall Keeble once said, "You know what 'status quo' means, don't you? It's Latin for the mess we're in!" Oh, how Keeble could get to the heart of the matter!

In His powerful Sermon on the Mount, Jesus appealed to the multitude to do three things. Let's listen to His words flowing across the pages and through the ages to us today:

> Ask, and it will be given to you; seek, and you will find; knock, and it will be opened to you. For everyone who asks receives, and he who seeks finds, and to him who knocks it will be opened (Matthew 7:7–8).

God has never lied to any of us. It is impossible for Him to lie (Hebrews 6:18). We can always take what He has to say to the bank. He is everything true and right and holy. When we ask God, He gives. When we seek God, we find Him. When we knock, He sends us our answers. You see, the Pearl Seeker wins every single time.

I must ask you again. Are you a Pearl Seeker? Let us pause, ponder, and examine our lives as we read these two passages once more:

> Seek the Lord and His strength; seek His face continually (Psalm 105:4).

> Again, the kingdom of heaven is like a merchant seeking fine pearls, and upon finding one pearl of great value, he went and sold all that he had and bought it (Matthew 13:45–46).

THE RELATIONSHIP

When we become Christians, God puts us into His church, His family (Acts 2:47). Here we belong and have a home. We women are no longer strangers but children of the Father. What a marvelous treasure we have found when we find God! The Pearl Seeker desires a relationship with God in His church.

The Pearl Seeker has a relationship with God that others will never understand, simply because they never truly desire that kind of relationship. Do you know what I am saying, girls? God tells us throughout the Bible, "Seek Me. You will find Me and I will bless you." The Bible is our treasure and God is our Pearl. "They who seek the Lord shall not be in want of any good thing" (Psalm 34:10).

So where do we go from here, my sweet sister? If a relationship is not growing, it is dying. There is a decision to be made: to grow or not to grow; to learn or to refuse to learn.

What will it be? Will you be a Pearl Seeker? Like the old hymn asks, "What will your answer be?"

There is much to be done, girls. There are people to be taught and helped; children to be loved and guided; older folks to be cherished and reminded of His love; a dying and lost world to be saved; teenagers to be listened to, but frankly warned. God's list goes on and on.

Each one of us is a work in progress. God isn't finished with us yet, is He? Let's read the Bible, learn, and grow while we have time. It certainly is true: "A mind is a terrible thing to waste." What a travesty it would be to not give our minds, our intellects, and our hearts back to the very one who created us—our Father in heaven. And what a travesty it would be if we didn't use them for our Father's work here on earth!

To the work, my sister! Redeem the time, and make the most of what is left. Life is short, and what, my sister, is more important in your life than God?

ALWAYS REMEMBER THIS

As we close this book, may I leave you with something from the bottom of my heart? I love you, and I am praying for you as you press on to know the Lord. "So let us know, let us press on to know the Lord. His going forth is as certain as the dawn; and He will come to us like the rain, like the spring rain watering the earth" (Hosea 6:3).

There is no greater calling or desire in the whole wide world; nothing is more worthy than being just a Christian, just a Pearl Seeker. Like the commercial says, "Priceless." Who in her right mind would ever regret knowing God or going to heaven?

Throughout my life, my mama had a habit of looking me in the eye—even when she had dementia and did not know my name—and saying, "I will meet you at the gate."

So, my sweet sisters, I say the very same thing to you now. I will meet you at the gate. Heaven's gate. Never, never, never give up on God. He is working in your life in ways you cannot even imagine. Have faith. Remember, we walk by faith and not by sight. Learn, learn, learn and grow, grow, grow. Don't turn back. Step over the line. Stay the course. Don't stop loving and don't stop seeking Him. He is waiting for you.

> The steadfast love of the Lord never ceases;
> His mercies never come to an end;
> They are new every morning;
> Great is your faithfulness.
> The Lord is my portion, says my soul,
> Therefore I will hope in him.
> The Lord is good to those who wait for him,
> To the soul who seeks him.
>
> —Lamentations 3:22–26 ESV

Be the Pearl Seeker, my sister; find the treasure. Be the soul that seeks Him. Oh, the blessings in store for you!

The Pearl Seeker

I stand at the ocean in amazement
Of what You have done for us all.
The sound of the waves,
The glimmer of the water,
The peace that always enthralls.

Tell me, O Lord, what you want of me.
Show me, my Father, and I will do.

The Pearl Seeker I am.
The Pearl Seeker I'll be
Until I get home to You.

—Becky Blackmon

Prayer: Lord, help me to seek to know that God is real.

Song: Do You Know My Jesus?

Have you a heart that's weary,
Tending a load of care?
Are you a soul that's seeking
Rest from the burden you bear?

Chorus:
Do you know my Jesus?
Do you know my friend?
Have you heard He loves you,
And that He will abide till the end?

Where is your heart, O pilgrim?
What does your light reveal?
Who hears your call for comfort
When naught but sorrows you feel?

Who knows your disappointments?
Who hears each time you cry?
Who understands your heartaches?
Who dries the tears from your eyes?

Digging for Pearls

1. Discuss the importance of trusting the Lord. (See Proverbs 3:5.)

2. What does God want from each of us?

3. What kind of relationship do you want to have with God?

4. List some results of allowing the Word of Christ to "richly dwell" in us (Colossians 3:16).

Works Cited

Chesser, Frank. *Thinking Right about God.* Huntsville, AL: Publishing Designs, Inc., 2014. Print.

Coffman, Burton. *Commentary on Ezra.* Web.

Coffman, Burton. *Commentary on Genesis.* Web.

Coffman, Burton. *Commentary on the Gospel of Matthew.* Abilene, TX: ACU Press, 1974. Print.

Coffman, Burton. *Commentary on Luke.* Abilene TX: ACU Press, 1984. p.64. Print.

Coffman, Burton. *Commentary on Proverbs 16.* Web.

Coffman, Burton. *Commentary on Psalms.* Web.

Fowler, Lea. *Precious Are God's Plans.* Abilene, TX: Quality Publications, 1986. Print.

Jackson, Wayne. *New Testament Commentary.* Stockton, CA: Christian Courier Publications, 2012. Print.

Johnson, Aubrey. *The Barnabas Factor.* Nashville, TN: Gospel Advocate Co., 2004. Print.

Sanders, Phil. *In Search of the Lord's Way.* Edmond, OK. May 3, 2015. Television.

Shank, Michael. *Muscle and a Shovel.* s.p. 2011. Print.

Sheerer, Jim. *New Testament Commentary.* Walton, KS: Yeoman Press, LLC, 2001. Print.

Tenny, Merrill C. *Zondervan Pictorial Bible Dictionary.* Nashville, TN: Southwestern Co. 1966. Print.

Turner, J. J. *Christians, Wake Up!* Huntsville, AL: Publishing Designs, Inc., 2012. Print.

Westcott, Brooke Foss. *The Epistle to the Hebrews,* 2nd edition. London: McMillan and Company, 1892. Print.